THE SECRETS OF
DR. KILLIECRANKIE

by

BRIAN J. SUMNER

RockMill
PUBLISHING

Rock Mill Publishing, P.O. Box 8243 Evansville, IN 47716, U.S.A.

First published in the United States of America by Rock Mill Publishing a company of Humble Planet Media Group, LLC. 2024

The Library of Congress Cataloging-in-Publication Data is available upon request.

ISBN 979-8-9917494-0-4 (Paperback)
ISBN 979-8-9917494-2-8 (Hardback)
ISBN 979-8-9917494-1-1 (EBook)

Printed in the United States of America
Set in Garamond
Designed by Ben Brock
Edited by Samantha Ripple

Dedication

For Crystal, I can never love you enough or thank you enough for always believing in me.

For Pops, you are always with me and I'd like to believe you would have loved this book.

Contents

THE SECRETS OF
DR. KILLIECRANKIE

Prologue

The heavy hum of the service truck filtered out amongst the trees of the darkly lit, Henderson backwoods. A small opening in the canopy above exposed the star-speckled sky, revealing a full moon.

The light from the moon fought to make its way down to the forest floor, but the branches would not relent as if mustering all of their will to protect the darkness from the impending light. The power of the moon was too great, in some aspects, as cascading light trickled down between the leaves and the branches creating the illusion of floating light while also projecting shadows that appeared to be as alive as the trees themselves.

The headlights on the truck were off, but the soft, red glow of the running taillights cast out an eerie, ambient light that forebode of something sinister taking place there on the dirty, grass-patched county road. This stretch of road had once been part of a much larger piece of property owned by the first generation of medical practitioners who went by the name of Killiecrankie.

Dr. Phillip Artemis Killiecrankie, Sr., PhD, had come to Henderson County in the latter part of the 1920s. Despite his rough upbringing on the streets of Old New York and his tumultuously abusive home life, Dr. Killiecrankie was able to put himself through medical school, after which, he quickly married. Then, without warning, the doctor unexpectedly decided to leave New York, abandoning his position at a prestigious medical facility, heading west and settling in Western Kentucky.

Some say it was to get away from the hustle and bustle of the biggest city in the country. However, there are rumors that his abrupt departure from The Big Apple may have been mingled with some unsavory business dealings linked to his medical practice at one of New York State's most prestigious medical facilities.

His origins at that time were unknown, but what is known is after arriving in Henderson, Kentucky, he went straight to work investing his savings into land prospecting and development. A large area just on the outskirts of town with plenty of trees, lakes, and countryside was of particular interest to him. It was far enough to avoid the hustle and bustle of a growing city. Or just far enough to not have locals looking into his affairs.

Over time, however, local authorities would take a very active interest in Dr. Killiecrankie's affairs pertaining to the sanatorium he established in the Spring of 1930. What had opened to a lot of fanfare and praise for such dedication to the continuing advancement in the field of mental well-being quickly devolved into a serious local emergency of the highest of criminal auspiciousness.

Rumors began to swirl in the community within a few years, of reports of patients being abused, physically and psychologically. Stories of malpractice and experimental treatments bordering on outright torture wafted out into the county's social circles. Of course, none of this was ever corroborated by evidence, and, despite the rumor mill working incessantly, it took decades before any real justice would think to come for the Killiecrankie family; but by then, the damage had been done.

Many patients, men and women alike, sometimes children, would bear the scars upon their bodies and their minds from the gregarious acts that took place beyond those walls. The next generation of Killiecrankie men became acolytes of Dr. Phillip Killiecrankie and his malicious experimentations that bordered on barbarianism. A gross and sinister family business that bore years of abuse and destruction of the human soul and spirit by way of manipulation, torture, and cruelty toward man.

As sinister as this place's mark on time had been, nothing could have prepared the community for what happened next, when, without warning or explanation, the sanatorium shut down.

Doors locked. Lights off. Quiet.

As if in one, quick instance, the staff and patients disappeared from existence. The authorities searched the premises and the surrounding grounds but to no avail. The patients had disappeared.

Months would turn into years before the truth of what happened to the patients would be unearthed, and, during that time, the sanatorium stood prominently on that county property.

Untouched. Vacant. Haunting.

The heavy thud of a foot, belonging to an imposing figure stepping out of the back of a service truck, imprinted the ground on the dirty, grass-patched county road. He walked slowly, without fear, through the dark shadows of the trees that towered above, methodically making his way into the overgrown brush alongside the road.

After about thirty yards, he found a beat-down, grass path, that meandered through the oaks and maple trees, plodding deeper into the dark forest. He continued his pace, unafraid of what lay ahead of him, as if he already knew what was out there.

He walked slowly for a few minutes before pausing in his stride to the sound of shuffling feet approaching from up ahead. Within a few moments, a small group of people, men, and women both emerged from the blackened abyss of the forest and froze in terror at the man that stood before them.

They were disheveled and a filthy mess with stringy hair and bad nutrition, and the clothes they wore were clearly hospital gowns of some type, though any markings or colors or identifiers of where they came from had been worn away long ago. The man in front of them stood still and stared intently at them.

They didn't scream. They didn't move. They held their breath.

A weighted breeze pushed through the canopy above, shifting the branches of the oaks and the maples, causing a chorus of clapping from the leaves that held tightly to their branch homes. The loose debris of dirt and crunchy, dead leaves on the forest floor acted like sheets of paper in a ticker-tape parade, dancing around the ankles of the unsanitary bunch who were frozen in fear on the path. The man stepped forward, slowly. He didn't speak.

The men and women did not move. They couldn't. Fear had them now. He calmly reached out his hand and held it out as an offering. The group did nothing. They couldn't.

A young woman toward the back of the group casually pushed her way through the crowded huddle, making her way toward the man. She stood in front of him, staring at what would be his face, though it was completely darkened by the shadows. She looked at his outstretched hand, placed her hand in his, and he turned and led her out of the forest. The rest of the group, now realizing he was there to help them, followed closely behind as they made their way up the path, back to the dirty, grass-patched road.

After loading everyone up in the back of the service truck, the man, without speaking, pointed toward the driver's seat, silently instructing the young woman to drive. She agreed, without saying a word. The man then climbed into the passenger seat of the service truck as a local radio station interrupted the music with an emergency bulletin...

"...This just in: a local health facility in Henderson County is now on complete lock-down after it's been reported that several of the mental health patients have escaped from the commons area of the facility. Workers responding to cries of help from fellow coworkers found the coworker

unconscious with heavy blood loss next to a window in the commons area that had been completely shattered. Officials are unsure at this moment of the total number of escaped patients as they are currently trying to get together a count for the number of patients on site. When they have any more information, they will let local authorities know, but, for now, officials at the Tranquil Meadows Health Facility are saying local residents should shelter in place, lock their doors, and if they see something suspicious, please do not hesitate to call the police. Of course, Tranquil Meadows Health, as most of us locals know, was established in 1973 by brothers Phillip and Morrison Killiecrankie who previously worked at the Western Kentucky Rehabili..."

The man lowered the volume of the radio and slowly turned his face toward the young woman. The colored glow of the dashboard lights illuminated the cab of the truck, revealing the man's face in a neon, nourishing fashion.

His skin was disfigured, and his hair was completely gone. A mask, reminiscent of a gas mask without filters, clung tightly around his mouth and nose. Metal attachments were embedded in various spots on his head which looked painful, but he never showed any evidence of that pain. His eyes were void of any life.

Dark. Endless. Soulless.

He breathed slowly, without any anxiety or stirring of emotion. He was calm. He looked at the young woman sitting next to him. She stared back, unafraid. Her hand slowly slid across the seat and she rested it on top of his. So much was said without a word being spoken and a plan was formulated without being verbalized.

The young woman applied the brake and engaged the service truck into drive. The brake lights blazed a blood-red glow, projected with prominence out onto the forest backdrop, turning the tall oaks and maple trees into giant, red nightmares. Just before the brake was released, the man with the mask glanced at the side mirror.

On the ground, highlighted by the eerie brake lights, the dead eyes of a man in a service uniform stared back at him, blood running from the large gash on his forehead, pooling up in a viscous puddle that appeared almost black in the shine of the bright brake lights. As the young woman slowly drove them away, deeper down the dirty, grass-patched road, the man with the mask looked ahead, unfazed by his work, and disappeared with his newly found companions of the night.

Chapter One
"Connections to the Past"

Sheriff's Office
July 21, 1986 | 8:00 A.M.

On any other hot, humid day in the middle of summer in Henderson County, Kentucky, not one person would pay much attention to a sleek, black, unmarked sedan rolling up into the space just outside the Sheriff's Office. However, locals will take notice when you exit that same vehicle and you're a man of above-average height, muscular build, and dressed to the nines in a stylish dark suit that clearly indicates an affiliation with a federal agency. No one wears a suit like that in this area during this time of year unless they're of some notable importance.

Special Agent Brandon Whittaker found himself traveling to an area of the country he was not familiar with, chasing down a lead that he hoped would help shed some light on particulars pertaining to highly irregular criminal activity outside of our nation's capital. He had been chosen by his superiors for this case due to his stellar record; he had spent the last two years hunting down high-level criminal threats notorious for the violent nature in which they committed their crimes.

SA Whittaker had been given the moniker of "The Philosopher" by his peers for how he would handle suspect interrogation, often sitting for hours in silence with a suspect, without so much as a "Hi, how are you?" or "Weather sure is nice today, huh?"

To those watching from behind the two-way glass, he appeared as if he was spending that time thinking about anything else other than the actual interrogation. It would be at that point, without warning, he would start throwing out facts to the suspect they thought no one else knew about!

Eventually, suspects would talk themselves into their arrest, leaving the interrogated suspect confused as to how this unsuspecting agent got the best of them. Taking an almost mentalist approach, Special Agent Brandon Whittaker quickly became the superstar of the Federal Bureau of Investigation.

The young agent, carrying only a briefcase, made his way into the Sheriff's office, removing his dark-shaded sunglasses as he stepped inside and was greeted by a welcome wave of air conditioning. A middle-aged woman with overly feathered hair sitting at the front receptionist's desk looked up from her notepad, made immediate eye contact, and greeted him with a smile.

"Hello young man, have you been helped yet?" she eagerly asked.

"No, ma'am, I haven't..." he replied as he stepped forward, removing his bureau-issued wallet and ID badge. "I'm Special Agent Brandon Whittaker with the FBI. I'm supposed to be having a meeting with..."

Before he could finish, a sheriff's deputy popped out from the side hallway and said, "SA Whittaker? I'm Deputy Martin with the Henderson County Sheriff's Office. If you come with me, we've been expecting you. Thank you, Louise." He nodded to the receptionist as he turned and quickly headed back down the hallway.

Deputy Martin was of average height and build and could probably blend into a crowd with ease, having no discerning physical attributes that made him stand out.

Whittaker nodded and smiled at Louise and followed Deputy Martin. Both men walked at a brisk pace down the hallway, around the corner, and into a small meeting room on the left. Inside at an oblong table, another sheriff's deputy was already sitting, reading the morning paper.

"Whittaker this is Deputy Harkins. He's been asked to sit in with us by Sheriff Dobson. Please take a seat." Deputy Martin grabbed the far seat at the table where a hefty file folder had been opened and sprawled out for viewing. Both SA Whittaker and Deputy Harkins shook hands, exchanged pleasantries, and then took their seats.

Deputy Harkins was young and built like an athlete. His chiseled face gave him a serious demeanor, though his voice was kind. Whittaker placed his briefcase on the table, which got a side glance from Martin.

"Sheriff Dobson should be here any moment, he's taking care of some last-minute issues in another department," said Deputy Martin as he read over a page from the case file on the table.

"I understand... a sheriff's job can be pretty hectic at times. I appreciate the courtesy your sheriff has extended on such short notice," said SA Whittaker.

Deputy Martin shifted in his seat, not making eye contact, almost annoyed by the presence of the young FBI agent. Whittaker glanced across the table to Deputy Harkins, looking for the possibility of small talk, but Harkins simply sat quietly. Whittaker smirked, deciding to just sit in silence till the Sheriff arrived.

After a few quiet minutes, Harkins cleared his throat and spoke, "So, Special Agent Whittaker... if you don't mind me asking, why are you here? I mean, the FBI? In Henderson, KY?"

Whittaker sat up, adjusted his jacket, and said, "I'll be happy to tell you why I'm here... when Sheriff Dobson joins us."

A breathy nasal laugh formed from the other end of the table where Deputy Martin was seated. He remained looking down at the file, and under his breath started talking, as if he were having a conversation with himself but was clearly directing it toward Special Agent Whittaker. "Little Po'Dunk, middle o'nowhere, Henderson County Sheriff's Deputies can't get the job done so big, bad Bureau Boy gotta come down and fix everything, I reckon..."

Whittaker laughed.

"Wait, were you brought in to help us on some cases, SA Whittaker? Is this about the disappearances?" asked Harkins.

"We don't need help, Harkins!" Deputy Martin barked back, finally looking up from his case file and staring a hole right through the young deputy. Harkins slunk back in his chair, mildly defeated but also annoyed at his partner.

Whittaker leaned forward, gently resting his palms on the table, "Look, it's obvious that you've been told that a 'Big Bad Bureau Boy' was being brought in, and it's even more obvious that neither of you know why I'm here."

"Why are you here?!" Martin snapped back, frustration written all over his face with this stranger coming into his house with not one inkling as to why.

As Whittaker was just about to respond, a booming voice from the hallway echoed through the doorway into the small meeting room, "Because he needs our help just as much as we need his help."

All three of the men immediately stood up and turned to see an older gentleman displaying the rank of sheriff on his uniform enter the room. His appearance was professional, and he carried himself well.

He walked straight to SA Whittaker with an extended hand, "Thank you for coming and I hope my department can be of some service to you. Gentlemen, please sit down, and let's get started."

Sheriff Dobson talked with the voice of a man who had experienced many different aspects of life. Be it as a soldier, a leader, or a public servant, when he spoke, you listened. After everyone got themselves comfortable, he quickly got everyone up to speed.

"I'm sorry I've been quite hush-hush with the details of the arrival of SA Whittaker but I felt, due to the circumstances of the case he has been tasked with, and its significance to us, that it would make more sense for him to explain the details himself. And let me just go ahead and put this out there right now to you two..." he motioned to his deputies, "… this will be a joint effort between our two agencies. You *will* assist SA Whittaker in *any* capacity he deems necessary. Am I clear on those two points?"

Both men silently nodded in agreement. Satisfied with their compliance, Sheriff Dobson turned to Whittaker and said, "Special Agent, please."

SA Whittaker nodded and stood up in front of the other three men and began to lay out his case. "Six days ago, in a quiet neighborhood on the outskirts of Fredericksburg, VA, in the middle of the night, a home invasion led to a brutal murder. Now, on the surface, you would probably think this isn't something that would end up on the radar of the FBI, a simple home invasion gone wrong, and you would be right in thinking that. However, when we found out who the victim was and the circumstances of his death, it immediately changed everything."

"Who was the victim, sir?" asked Deputy Harkins.

"Former Colonel Will Braxton," Whittaker replied.

"A military man? Just horrible..." said Harkins.

The young deputy was fresh out of the army when he applied for a position with the sheriff's office. Though he never saw any live combat, he was proud of his service in the armed forces.

Harkins took a beat, then asked, "You said the circumstances of his death brought this case on your radar.

What were those circumstances?"

"Well, aside from the fact it's the death of a highly-decorated war veteran who continued his working relationship with the military via the private sector after retiring early from the military, it's the detail this was carried out by a group of people, not just one person. Three, maybe four people. The wife of Colonel Braxton couldn't say for certain due to the fact that the couple was startled awake by this group so early in the morning hours. Mrs. Braxton was led away from the house to the couple's car where one of the assailants put her in the back seat, tied her hands behind her back, and then drove her out into the middle of nowhere and left her," SA Whittaker explained.

"Wait... the perp just left her? Didn't assault her? Didn't murder her? Just left her?" asked Deputy Martin.

"That's correct. What's even more notable is that there doesn't seem to be a motive for burglary. Nothing was taken from the premises, and all of the couple's credit cards and cash are accounted for. According to Mrs. Braxton's statement, three or four people, she couldn't be certain if they were all men or men *and* women, woke her and her husband up around 2:15 am by placing duct tape over their mouths. Amidst her awakened slumber, she was quickly removed from the bedroom by a man in his mid to late thirties with stringy long hair, wearing what appeared to be a very worn and dingy medical gown. From what she could recollect, everyone in the room was in a medical gown of the same condition, except for one person who had a hooded jacket on and was facing away from her. The man who took her from the room then forced her into their own car, drove her forty-five minutes out of the city, pulled over, took the keys from the ignition, and split. She was so terrified that he was going to kill her that she closed her eyes and started praying and didn't open her eyes for a good fifteen minutes before she felt comfortable enough to look and see if he was still there. When Mrs. Braxton realized he was gone, she immediately untied herself and flagged down the next passing car. She hitched a ride to the nearest payphone and alerted the authorities."

"Clearly, this group of individuals was targeting the former colonel and needed to get the wife away from the scene to do so without her being able to identify anyone later during a potential lineup," Sheriff Dobson observed.

"Precisely," Whittaker said. "The only person she could ID with any certainty was the man who took her from her home. We were able to track this man down, seventy-five miles away, walking alone on a back county road. He did not resist at all but also never said a word during his arrest and initial interrogation. He's under tight lock and key, but he isn't talking at all, not even to his court-appointed attorney. Fingerprints traced him back to a mental facility just outside of Fredericksburg where he escaped, along with three other patients."

The deputies seemed to perk up at that last bit of news. "Well, there ya go! There's where your group of assailants came from. Pretty open and shut case if you ask me," Deputy Martin quipped.

Whittaker smirked. "If only, right? Too bad for us that the other three patients he escaped with were apprehended and placed back into the care of the facility within two hours of their escape. This fourth man, one of the suspects in my case, Darrell Bowldry, has been in and out of several mental facilities along the East Coast for the better part of the last six years. Whoever the other people were in the group that targeted Colonel Braxton came from somewhere else," he said. "It's also important to note that these people never spoke. Not one word was said during any of the encounters that the couple had with these people. Obviously, we can't say if anything was said to the Colonel in his final moments in his bedroom, but we are for sure certain that some kind of message was given to him that night," said Whittaker.

"What does that mean, 'a message'? What was the cause of death?" asked Martin.

"He was beaten to death with a leather strap," Sheriff Dobson chimed in.

Deputy Martin's eyes got significantly bigger as if he'd heard of this method before.

"More specifically, he had been beaten to the point of blood loss and the skin was completely ripped from his back. Early forensics reports suggest he was beaten unconscious, revived, and then beaten again until he passed. Now, in my short career with the bureau, I've seen and heard some pretty crazy cases. In fact, we've got a bit of a head-scratcher happening right now up in Hawkins that we can't make heads or tails of, but murder cases are typically straightforward once you figure out the motive. However, this case is of the most irregular sort in the sense that it seems our suspects are wanting us to solve this case."

The deputies looked confused. "How is that, sir?" asked Harkins.

Whittaker stepped to his briefcase. As he opened it, he spoke, "Due to the fact that our multiple suspects did a number of things that would indicate they have no intention of hiding from what they're doing. Not only did they leave a witness alive and then allow one of their group to be apprehended, but they also left behind the murder weapon and blatantly left behind a clue."

Whittaker had retrieved an evidence bag from his briefcase that had a solitary sheet of paper that appeared to have a bloody handprint on the page. Both deputies stood up to get a closer look, staring at the hand print, and began reading the text on the page.

"From the Office Archives of Dr. Phillip Artemis Killiecrankie, Sr., PhD," Harkins read aloud from the page. Deputy Martin's jaw dropped.

Whittaker continued, "Our investigation indicates that one person was responsible for the assault while at least two others watched and when the act was completed, this page was pressed into the bloody, skinned back of Colonel Braxton. The page seems to be from the file of a patient who stayed at the Western Kentucky Rehabilitation and Sanatorium sometime in either the sixties or seventies. There is no name on the file page, just a patient designation of Patient H7-423. I'm guessing Dr.

Killiecrankie took care of this patient in some capacity."

"I don't understand. Who is Dr. Phillip Killiecrankie?" asked Harkins.

"Are you kidding me, right now?" exclaimed Deputy Martin. "The asylum? The loony bin? The freakin' doctor who tortured all those patients years ago?"

"Sir, I grew up across the river in Evansville. I don't know about any of that," Harkins replied.

"Well, don't feel bad, Harkins," said Whittaker. "I didn't know about it either, but when we found this piece of paper stuck to our victim, I went into our database at the bureau and cross-referenced Dr. Phillip Killiecrankie, Sr. with Colonel Braxton, and guess what I discovered?" He paused dramatically. "Nothing...."

The deputies had been waiting for a big reveal, only to receive disappointment, until SA Whittaker began speaking again. "That is to say that I found nothing that would help me. I did, however, discover that there are records on file that contain references to both men. The only problem is, they are classified 'Top Secret due to National Security' and cannot be accessed by me without top-level military clearance," he added. "I also found a pretty hefty file kept by the bureau on Dr. Killiecrankie with about 90% of it redacted. However, I was able to run several patient and associate names in the file only to find an alarming number of disappearances associated with the good doctor and his facility throughout the years. The regularity of disappearances and how these disappearances occurred caused me to try and connect a very big hypothetical set of dots."

"Hypothetical, how? What do you mean?" asked Harkins.

"I made an imaginary line from Henderson, Kentucky to Washington, D.C. and decided to check to see how many mental health institutions were along the way. There's more than you would even care to think. Then I checked each facility to see how many of them had an uptick in attempted escapes over the last five years. About fifteen of them saw an alarming increase in patient volatility and attempted escapes. The number of successful escapes would make your skin crawl," said Whittaker, as the deputies looked on in disbelief.

"So naturally, finding this file page stuck to the dead colonel with the name of a doctor from this area seemed to be the only logical destination to begin my investigation. I reached out to your sheriff, here, to get some info on Dr. Killiecrankie and the asylum, and after a long, revelatory phone call last night, I am here to build my case and hopefully get some answers as to why a murder in Fredericksburg, Virginia is related to a defunct asylum in Henderson, Kentucky. I imagine a lot of what I'm looking for is sitting in that folder you've been gawking over ever since I got here, Deputy Martin," Whittaker pointed to the collection of file pages on the table in front of the listening deputy.

"Namely, the alarming number of mental health facility patients that have disappeared from this area dating back to the 1960s. Or maybe a handful of residents from this area who went missing only to be discovered later, beaten so badly by a leather strap that their skin fell off before they died. Or possibly the couple of residents who went missing as well, only to be discovered that they asphyxiated on some sort of deadly chemical pathogen that basically burned their airways from the inside out."

Deputy Martin calmly stacked all the pages back into the file folder and obligingly slid the file to Whittaker.

He then spoke, "So what are you trying to tell us, SA Whittaker? Is there some kind of cult made up of escaped crazy patients behind all this out there killing people for fun? Doesn't seem like the type of people who could organize something like this."

Sheriff Dobson stood up from the table and looked at Whittaker, "Tell them what you told me."

Special Agent Whittaker placed the files and the bloody page of evidence back into his briefcase. As he snapped the clasps back in place, he looked at the deputies and said, "Whoever these people are, they've got someone helping them. They're doing this for a reason... a purpose... and they're just getting started, because on the wall above Colonel Braxton's body, the killer used the colonel's blood to leave a note for the police." Both deputies remained still.

"It said..."

"Your sins will soon be on display"

Chapter Two
"Contractual Obligations"

Western Kentucky Rehabilitation and Sanitarium
September 20, 1961 | 10:37 A.M.

The leaves had begun to separate from the giant oaks and maples of the dense forest that lined the short meadow just outside the east wall of the Western Kentucky Sanitarium. Fall would soon blanket the area with cool, crisp air, erasing any signs of the hot, humid, summer days that annually baked the local residents.

During the summer, if you were to drive on the main highway, you would never know the sanatorium was even out there with all the trees blocking your sight. But during fall and winter, if you looked hard enough, you could make out the roof of the large building amidst the bare trees, backlit by a sky packed with precipitous clouds.

Nestled on the outskirts of Henderson, Kentucky, in a very picturesque snapshot of rural country America, the facility had been built to address the growing concern of mental instability of the general public of the tri-state area. A generation of people swallowed up in the burden of the financial relapse of the Great Depression and spurned on by civil and patriotic duty to their country in wartime, had started to feel their emotional and mental walls collapsing.

In the spring of 1930, hope came in the form of the Western Kentucky Rehabilitation and Sanitarium. A facility that was state of the art for its time and was poised to be the beacon of mental well-being for not only the residents of Kentucky, Indiana, and Illinois but would also stand tall as a 'light in the darkness of night' for those brave men returning home from war who weren't quite the same as when they left.

The land for the facility had been acquired sometime in 1928 and ground was broken in late summer of 1929. Overseeing the construction of the facility was the man who acquired the land rights and gave the proposal to the county: Dr. Phillip Artemis Killiecrankie, Sr., PhD. He had come from New York City, and set up an office and a home in the area, though no one could understand why he chose this area for he had neither relatives nor official ties to the area. However, all speculation was put aside once the announcement of the sanatorium hit all the papers in the region.

The residents of Henderson County felt a change for the better was coming, and they couldn't have been happier. Unfortunately, for the next three decades, the luster of the sanatorium and the hope it brought wore off for the locals. Stories and legends of what took place behind the walls of the sanatorium became the stuff of nightmares as tall tales were passed around by local yokels looking to stir the pot or hooligan school children trying to scare their friends.

Throughout the years, countless complaints were filed by many of the residents who had lived in the area since well before the erection of the sanatorium and even more complaints came from residents who had moved to the area in the years after its inception. Complaints of loud noises and screams echoing through the countryside all hours of the night, with the occasional escaped patient wandering through pastures and fields, only to be found the next day hiding in a barn, much to the surprise of the owners.

Over time, many people who had been patients in the facility often spoke of extreme behavioral changes and shifts in the demeanor of patients who had an extended stay at the sanatorium.

Complaints were logged and filed with the Sheriff's Office of patients who had undergone odd experimentations while sedated and of mysterious disappearances of patients who were seen on the grounds one day and gone the next. Odd occurrences seemed to be happening at the facility at an alarming rate over the decades of its existence, but local authorities were never able to do anything about any of these complaints because there was never any proof of ill-mannered medical malfeasance.

During this period, a large number of the residents speculated that the Sheriff's Office had some kind of "under the table" deal in place with Dr. Killiecrankie, allowing officials to look the other way whenever sketchy issues would be brought to the attention of the police. There were also theories about Dr. Killiecrankie being a bloodthirsty, maniacal doctor who was using patients to carve up and satiate his blood lust, then would use the scraps to feed his children! The rumor mill was always churning and never failed to pump out some entertaining fodder for people to talk about to amuse themselves.

One thing that did happen that could not be doubted was the arrival of a solid black, Lincoln Continental, one September morning. The car had US Military insignias and American flags affixed to the hood on either side, clearly marking its importance.

The sanatorium had been known to take in servicemen to help in their health and rehab, so that was not out of the ordinary, but a car like that in this area in 1961 immediately stuck out to the locals. The Continental came to a slow stop at the main entrance as an older gentleman with thinning white hair that was brushed straight back came carefully down the steps of the entrance to greet the visitor. The driver of the Continental, a younger-looking man in a well-pressed military uniform, came around the backside of the vehicle, nodding to the older man, then briskly opening the rear passenger door and immediately standing at attention. From the interior emerged a shorter man with a stocky build wearing a multitude of military decorations. He had darker skin and light brown hair, and he wore an expression that meant business.

"Good morning, Dr. Killiecrankie," he said in a "straight to the point" fashion.

"Good morning, Major Braxton," responded Dr. Killiecrankie, which seemed to frustrate his guest.

"Jesus H. Christ, Phillip, are you ever going to learn to read ranks? I'm a Lieutenant Colonel, now!" he snapped back while pointing to his newly acquired ranking.

Slightly amused, Dr. Killiecrankie gave a half attempt at a salute and said, "My apologies Lieutenant Colonel Braxton. May I get you a cup of coffee, Lieutenant Colonel Braxton?"

The Lieutenant Colonel was not amused. "You should probably watch your tone with me right now, Doc. I'm not in the mood for games. Aside from having to come all the way out here to this god-forsaken state and to your god-forsaken house of horrors, I've got the brass halfway up my keister about your little arrangement here...."

Killiecrankie moved closer, making a shushing motion with his finger to his lips as he politely escorted the Lt. Colonel a few steps away from a staff worker caring for a couple of patients in a nearby courtyard.

Braxton continued. "And they feel they've been more than accommodating for what little they've got in return. Sure, you've helped take care of a lot of enlisted men over the years, and the United States Military thanks you for that, but that's, ultimately, not what you were signed on for. Between the Virginia fiasco back in '43 and the fifty soldiers you almost killed in '58 with your little neuro-serum experiments, I gotta tell you, Doc, they're not happy with your results. Or should I say, the lack of results."

"You wanna keep your voice down when there's staff around, Lt. Colonel? That's not exactly public knowledge and you know that!" Dr. Killiecrankie was whispering as loud as he could to make his point to the Lt. Colonel. "Why are you even here? I didn't expect you for another two weeks, and why are you here during the day? Nighttime hours, Braxton. Nighttime hours. You wanna know why? So no one sees you here, that's why!"

"Look, I don't know how you did things with Major Jasper all those years before I took over, but I'm done with your little cloak and dagger BS, alright. I'll come when I damn well feel, and I didn't feel like making it a 'nightcap' this time around, okay? You got a problem with that arrangement, then I suggest you take it up with my boss…Oh, wait! My boss doesn't care about your little requests; he only cares about results. Which is why I'm here... results. Just remember, we may have come to you first, but you made assurances to us, and we expect you to follow through." said the Lt. Colonel as he smugly reached out and adjusted Dr. Killiecrankie's tie for him.

The doctor was visibly uncomfortable with Braxton touching his tie as he responded, "You and your superiors do realize that what I do isn't something that just happens overnight, right? Especially while running a full-time mental health facility that does actual work for the citizens in this county. My research and my procedures take time to develop. I am working nonstop, day and night, trying to break hundreds of years of medical monotony to give *your* boss, *your* superiors, and *your* military the edge it needs on the battlefield from the cutting-edge medical advancement that is being sought out behind these walls. We're making history here. What part of that do you not understand?"

"In case you haven't put two and two together, Phillip, the US Military Complex in partnership with the United States Government couldn't care less about making medical history or cementing your legacy in the medical field, which, let's be honest, that's what all this is really about for you." Lt. Col. Braxton said as Dr. Killiecrankie rolled his eyes.

He continued, "All we're interested in is recouping what is owed to us based on an agreement in a signed contract that you have with the United States Military. What part of *that* do *you* not understand?"

Dr. Killiecrankie stood for a moment, quiet and frustrated, planning his next words carefully to the Lt. Colonel. He took a breath and then said, "I fully understand my arrangement with the military...."

Braxton cut him off, "Contractual obligations."

"...fine, contractual obligations. But the reality is, I can't give the US Military what I don't have. I need more time," he said.

Braxton seemed slightly irritated as he looked around to make sure no one was within earshot. Satisfied that no one was listening, he leaned into Dr. Killiecrankie and asked, "Are you intentionally trying to sandbag the United States Military, Phillip?"

Confused, Dr. Killiecrankie responded, "Sandbag?"

"As in feeding me a lie? You're standing here telling me you have nothing to share with me today, but I have received no less than four calls to my office within the last week from your oldest son, Phillip Jr., stating that your work has had a major breakthrough and that someone associated with the partnership should get down to Kentucky post-haste to discuss next steps," said Braxton.

Dr. Killiecrankie's eyes grew bigger, and a scowl formed on his face.

"Judging by your reaction, this is a development you weren't quite prepared for, huh?"

"Obviously not," said Killiecrankie. With hands on hips, he paced slowly in a circle, staring off at the serene meadow that stretched out toward the forest at the far end of the property. "My son has spoken out of place, and I shall have a conversation with him later this afternoon. That being said, yes. I have had a breakthrough. And I didn't alert you of this breakthrough because, as I said previously, when you're working with research of the medical kind, time is a necessary part of the process. I still need more time, but since you are here, I might as well bring you up to speed."

Dr. Killiecrankie motioned to the front entrance of the Sanatorium, inviting Lt. Col. Braxton to follow him inside. The two men made their way up the steps, continuing through the entrance foyer, down a short hallway to the left, and into an interior office.

Inside, sitting at a desk in the corner, a beautiful, younger woman wearing a nurse's outfit was reading over a thick, opened, patient file. She looked up, seeing Lt. Col. Braxton, and immediately stood to greet the guest.

"Lt. Col. Braxton, this is Nurse Abigail Rucker. She has been assisting me in my research pertaining to the 'contractual obligations' we were discussing earlier. She is well-versed in the details of the said agreement and can be trusted...so, feel comfortable to speak freely in her presence. Nurse Rucker, do you have the file for Patient H7-25?"

"Yes, Doctor. I was just reading over the notes of our last session with him," she said as she turned back to the desk and retrieved the file.

As she handed the thick folder to Dr. Killiecrankie, he said, "Thank you, Nurse. Now, will you please gather up Patient H7 and bring him to Observation Room 2? Lt. Col. Braxton and I will join you in a few minutes.

She nodded in compliance and quickly left the room.

As she left, Braxton smirked and said, "Pretty girl, Phillip. I see why you hired here."

"She was hired to take care of my wife, Alesta," he quickly responded while thumbing through the file for Patient H7.

Not buying the answer, Braxton responded, "Oh sure, sure. I'm fairly confident that run-of-the-mill nurses hired to care for dementia patients are all the time finding themselves suddenly a major player in a contract with the US Military."

Agitated by the Lt. Col., Dr. Killiecrankie quickly closed the file in his hand. He then made intense eye contact and said, "Nurse Rucker has proven incredibly invaluable to me over the past decade. Not only has she helped with the care of my ailing wife, she has also implemented new healthcare methods and procedures for dealing with the more aggressive patients we see behind these walls, not to mention she brings an alternative approach and viewpoint to my research which helps make my work easier and more fruitful concerning breakthroughs. Literally, without her, my work here is dead in the water. So, you will show her the respect she has earned."

Braxton gave a huge smile, smacked Dr. Killiecrankie on the shoulder, and said, "Don't worry, Doc. I'll treat your girlfriend with the utmost respect."

Killiecrankie huffed and made his way out into the hallway with Braxton following close behind.

The two men walked in stride with each other down a well-lit corridor, passing a mid-sized recreation area and a couple of common rooms where various patients were sitting in wheelchairs and at card tables looking at books and magazines. Some patients were staring off at the ceiling, others were sprawled out on the floor playing with wooden blocks and tinker toys, and a few sat quietly on small couches talking to themselves.

The men turned a corner, passing a couple of patient rooms, then stopped at a room with a large glass window marked "Observation 2" on the door. Lt. Col. Braxton peered in through the window.

Inside, Nurse Rucker was seated at a white table, talking and holding hands with a small child in a patient's gown. The child was sitting patiently, rocking his legs back and forth.

"This is the big breakthrough? A child?" scoffed Braxton.

"All is not what it seems, Lt. Col," responded Killiecrankie as he reopened the file, reading some notes.

"What is he... five years old?!"

"Six," laughed Killiecrankie. "Actually, he just had a birthday."

Braxton was not amused but didn't immediately dismiss the doctor. "I don't know what this is, but it better not be a waste of my time. Where are his parents?"

Killiecrankie looked up from the file into the room where the patient and Nurse Rucker were sitting. He paused for what seemed an abnormally long second and then responded, "No parents, Lt. Col."

Braxton gave him a quick look.

"... Let's just say this child is a volunteer."

As Braxton stepped away from the glass, he glanced down at the file, reading the front cover as Dr. Killiecrankie held it in his hands. "No patient name? Just H7-25?"

The doctor held up the file to Braxton and explained the numbered designation. "When I started this program, I needed a way to keep track of my progress. I didn't want to be burdened by the personal aspects of the patients like you said, just the results. So, each patient was treated in succession. The first patient was A. Then the second was B... and so on and so on...."

"What does the '7' indicate?" asked Braxton.

"Cycles. It indicates I'm on the seventh cycle of the alphabet. So Patient H7 here is the seventh H I've had in this facility. Understand?" explained Killiecrankie, opening the file and returning his focus to the notes.

"What happened to the patients from the earlier cycles?" asked Braxton.

Coldly, Killiecrankie did not respond to this question.

Braxton stood silent for a moment, processing the meaning of the numbers then asking, "Do I even want to know what the '25' means?"

Without looking up, Killiecrankie responded in a very dry tone, "Experimentations."

Even Lt. Col. Braxton was taken aback by this revelation. Patient H7 had been experimented on twenty-five times, and he was only six years old. The facts laid upon Braxton gave him a moment to pause, but the sticker shock quickly wore off as Killiecrankie closed the file and then nodded for him to follow into the Observation Room.

As Dr. Killiecrankie and Lt. Col. Braxton stepped into the room, Nurse Rucker stood up and made her way toward the door. She paused at the doctor, gently placing her hand on his arm, and said,

"If you need me, I'll be right outside in the hallway, Doctor." He nodded, and she promptly left, with Braxton looking on and taking note of the small exchange.

Killiecrankie sat at the table in the seat next to Patient H as Braxton remained standing in the corner closest to the door. No one said a word and the silent seconds grew to minutes with Dr. Killiecrankie and Patient H staring at each other. Braxton shifted from leg to leg as he leaned against the glass window in the corner, checking his watch every fifteen seconds or so, waiting impatiently for something to happen.

After another few moments of silence, Dr. Killiecrankie let out a soft chuckle and said, "You're not wrong!" Killiecrankie leaned back in his seat and opened the file while Braxton just looked on confused.

"What do you mean 'You're not wrong.' What are you talking about?" he asked.

"Patient H7 was just telling me that you look like a meanie," explained the doctor.

Braxton became even more confused and agitated because nothing had been said. "What are you talking about? The kid never said a word."

Another brief moment of silence passed and then Killiecrankie said to Patient H7, "You're right about that." The doctor couldn't help but snicker.

At this point, Lt. Col. Braxton had seen enough and was furious. "You know what Doc, I've had enough of the games, alright," he stood up straight, taking a step toward the table and addressing the doctor directly.

"I don't know what type of juvenile BS you've got going on here between you and your sons helping you run this place, but I don't appreciate coming here and having my chain yanked, you got me?"

"Sir, please... you don't understa-"

"I am a decorated United States Military veteran, highly ranked for my service to my country...."

"No, no, he's not mad at you," Killiecrankie said to Patient H7 who hadn't said a word. "Sir..."

"...And I have been put into a position to oversee the progress of a secret program by our government that is supposedly in place to help save the lives of thousands of soldiers who enlist in our armed forces, but all I see is a man who has taken advantage of the very contract he has entered into agreement with..."

"Sir, please, I need you to calm down..."

Patient H7 began to shift in his seat, furled brow and eyes laser focused on the Lt. Colonel.

"...A MAN WHO SPOUTS OFF ABOUT MEDICAL BREAKTHROUGHS BUT HAS YET TO PRODUCE A SINGLE SHRED OF MEDICALLY RELEVANT EVIDENCE, DESPITE BURNING THROUGH FINANCIAL MILITARY CAPITAL!!"

The Lt. Col. was yelling at this point. Outside in the hall, Nurse Rucker looked on worried.

Down the corridor, other patients could be heard becoming agitated.

Killiecrankie's attention was on Patient H7.

"No, Patient H, it's okay. It's okay. Sir, you have to calm down, ple-"

"...YOU ARE NO DOCTOR! YOU'RE A MAN PRETENDING TO BE SOMETHING HE'S NOT, USING THIS PLACE TO LIVE OUT YOUR SICK, TWISTED FANTASIES ALL ON THE DIME OF THE US MILITARY, BUT IT STOPS, RIGHT NOW!"

Braxton turned to make his way toward the door when out of nowhere, an ominous, booming voice manifested inside his head saying the word,

"STOP!"

The sound rattled inside his head, reverberating in his very core, while the force sent him tumbling back against the glass window behind him, snapping it in place and creating a spider effect along the length of the frame. The Lt. Col. hit the ground hard, grabbing both sides of his head with his hands, breathing heavily, and trying to process what had just happened to him.

Dr. Killiecrankie stood up and turned to Patient H7 and exclaimed, "NO, NO, PATIENT H! We do not do that here, remember?!"

He then turned his attention to Braxton, who had made it back to his feet and was, staggering in the corner.

"Will, are you okay?"

Braxton was dazed and immediately felt a military instinct to evacuate from the threat.

Without saying a word, he made his way to the doorway and was met by Nurse Rucker rushing into the room. She bypassed the Lt. Col. and went straight to the young boy and began to comfort him.

Killiecrankie followed Braxton into the hallway.

Lt. Col. Braxton took huge breaths and undid his tie as he stood outside the room in the long corridor. Killiecrankie stood with him and tried to help him calm down.

"Will... come on, Will, talk to me. Are you okay?

Braxton stood up straight, still breathing heavily, composed, but still very much unnerved.

"What in the exact hell was that?!"

Killiecrankie smirked. "That is what happens when you agitate a person who has an underdeveloped and uncontrollable ability of telepathy," responded Killiecrankie.

Braxton took a beat to fully understand what Phillip Killiecrankie said to him and then, through his deep breaths, started to laugh softly.

"Telepathy? Are you serious right now, Doc?" he asked, already knowing the answer from what he had just witnessed. "This is truly real?"

Killiecrankie smiled, nodded his head, and motioned for the Lt. Col. to move down the hall, out of earshot of the young boy.

"It's very much real, Lt. Col. But it's also very much in its adolescence. What you just experienced, I experienced about three months ago by complete accident. Ever since then, Nurse Rucker and I have been cultivating his ability. Not pushing too hard. My god, he's only six, and he can already do this, but think about how great his ability will be if we give him more time to develop. He needs more time. *I* need more time...."

Braxton had fully composed himself by this time. He casually walked along the glass window, staring into the room where Nurse Rucker was seated in a chair next to the young boy, arms around him while he cried, comforting him and letting him know that he did nothing wrong.

Braxton turned back to the doctor, "How is this possible? I know you have theories. How? Right now, tell me everything..."

Killiecrankie went back into the room and gathered up the file and its contents from the table. On his way out, he said something to Nurse Rucker and then stepped back into the hall. Braxton watched the exchange.

Returning to the hall, Killiecrankie opened the file and began to speak.

"From a chemical standpoint, Patient H is no different than any other little boy living out in the world. If he gets a cut, he bleeds, he heals. If he's sick, he feels bad, he heals. His growth rate is that of a normal child, and his aptitudes are normal base-level readings, as well. But what makes him stand out above everyone else is his blood. His blood is not a normal blood type. In fact, his blood doesn't even register against all known blood types. From a vascular standpoint, he's the 'Anomaly of all Anomalies.'

Braxton's eyes could not hold back his newfound excitement, though he desperately tried to play it cool in front of the doctor.

After a contemplative pause, he asked, "Scientifically speaking, what makes his blood so unique? More importantly, how does his blood correlate to what just happened in this room?"

"His blood doesn't operate the same as a normal person's blood. When the heart pumps blood out, it's reintroducing fresh, clean blood that delivers new oxygen to the cells in the body, helping to keep you alive. Patient H7's heart does that same function; however, his blood not only carries fresh oxygen, it also carries an advanced chemical property that produces electromagnetic pulse signatures. These signatures are constantly sending electrical signals through the bloodstream directly to the brain. I mean, it's unprecedented what his blood is doing. Incredibly rare. I've only seen it one other time. We as humans can only access a small percentage of brain function, but his blood allows him to access parts of his brain that no one has ever thought could be possible. We just had to figure out a way to make that signal known to Patient H7 so that he could learn to access it and use it. What happened to you today happened to me when we tried electro-shock therapy on him. The electricity introduced into his system caused the blood to move so rapidly and become so electrically charged that it was essentially attacking the inside of his body to get out!"

"My god," Braxton reacted upon hearing this recount of Patient H7's medical history. "So, while he was defending himself against the treatment, his body was unknowingly unlocking an ability that he had no idea he was even capable of?"

"Exactly!" responded Killiecrankie. "Pain Induced DNA Evolution. It's what I've been theorizing since my time in New York and through all my work for your military. Those medical breakthroughs I've been chasing and was preaching about earlier... this is it. This is the next evolutionary step. We've found it!"

Braxton took a beat then asked, "You said you've only ever seen blood like his once before. Whose blood?"

Killiecrankie paused. "I'd like to keep that confidential at this time."

Braxton didn't budge. "It's the mother's blood, isn't it? You said this kid is here as a volunteer but he's six, and you're full of crap, so, shoot straight with me right here, right now. Who is the kid's mother?"

Killiecrankie unwittingly glanced through the window to Nurse Rucker then looked back at Braxton and said, "I can't tell you that information at this time."

Braxton gave a heavy sigh and said, "You just did, Doc. I guess you weren't lying when you said without her your research is dead in the water."

After a brief pause, Braxton realized the child and his mother and asked, "Who is the father?"

Killiecrankie didn't respond.

"Ah, Jesus, Phillip!" Braxton exclaimed as he stepped away from the doctor.

The picture being painted told the story of a child born into a world of experimentation for the gain of others. The idea of love for this child was never an ideal or an option. It was always about the results and what this child could offer beyond the walls that contained him. He had been born to serve a purpose that was not his own. Only time would be able to tell the ramifications of this conceit. Lt. Col. Braxton stood at the doorway of the observation room, thinking carefully about what his next move was.

After a few moments of reflection, Killiecrankie stood next to him and asked, "Well?"

Braxton leaned over to Killiecrankie to whisper in his ear.

"Does the child know who his parents are?"

"No! Of course not! There's nothing to gain from him knowing that," responded Killiecrankie.

"Good. Keep it that way," said Braxton as he fixed his tie and straightened up his uniform. "The next step for you, I imagine, is to bring this fine young man to the brass up in Washington for a little demonstration!"

"What? No! I told you, this is too early. *I* need more time," cried Killiecrankie.

Nurse Rucker and Patient H7 could now hear the commotion and turned to see the two men debating.

"What did I say when I first got here, Doc? Results. We have been waiting for results and look here, you delivered," he stated, pointing to Patient H7.

He then said to the young child, "Don't worry about before, son! Not your fault! Very impressive!"

Killiecrankie was increasingly frustrated at this point.

Braxton then said, "Can you imagine if we were able to take this young boy to war-torn areas where we have Military Personnel stationed, and he could just mow right through the enemy's presence with a single thought! Can you imagine the number of soldiers' lives we could save with him? Like all this hubbub down in Cuba or over in Southeast Asia? The possibilities are endless."

Killiecrankie had had enough at this point. "That's not going to happen right now, Braxton! He's not ready for that."

"Oh, we'll see about that, Doc. What if we just go ahead

and shut down your little operation you've got going and expose every little thing you've done to get where you are? Hm? You forget who you're in business with? The military and the government have an uncanny knack for making things go away when necessary. You don't play ball, we can make this all go away. It would be a shame if somehow all of your sins were suddenly put on display for the world to see," said Braxton.

"My sins? Anything and everything I've ever done behind these walls has been for the advancement of medicine. In the name of science and discovery, what I do has meaning and value. Yes, the ends do justify the means. Always have! Talk about my sins? What about yours, Lt. Col.? You hide behind valor and use it as a mask to show the world how righteous you are, yet here you are, behind the scenes, using my work to make your job of killing as efficient as possible. Oh no, your sins have always been on display. The difference between you and me is that the bodies I stack up will always amount to medical progress while the bodies you stack are just a stark reminder of just how mentally unevolved we are as a society. My work advances the human spirit, your work crushes it."

Both men stood there in the doorway, staring each other down, neither one refusing to back away.

After a few tense moments, Braxton gave a crooked smile and said, "You have one year. I'll keep this quiet for now and let the higher-ups know that you're 'doing some really fine work' and 'our taxpayer dollars are going to a good cause', that sort of thing. One year. You, better make this fully functional or the military will not make this comfortable for you. Understand?"

Killiecrankie nodded.

"I'll show myself out, doc." Lt. Col. Braxton quietly made his way down the corridor and out of sight.

Nurse Rucker stood up from the table, leaving Patient H7 sitting and watching, and made her way into the hallway where Dr. Killiecrankie was still standing, in deep thought. She glanced at the young child and then moved Killiecrankie away from the doorway to the far end of the hall near a set of unused office spaces. She was very much interested in what the Lt. Col. learned from his conversations with Killiecrankie.

"What all did you tell him," she asked.

"He knows..." Killiecrankie immediately responded.

"What do you mean 'He knows'? What does he know?" she frantically asked.

"About us. About him. He was able to put it together. He may be a jerk, but he didn't get where he is by being an idiot. The only solace I'm taking from this is that he isn't going to use it against us. He knows we're the parents, but he also knows what Patient H7 is capable of, so we have that working for us for now," he responded, trying to smooth the situation over. Nurse Rucker seemed disgruntled.

"You can call him by his real name instead of Patient H7," she said.

"No, I can't. And neither should you. We created him for the purpose of this program. He is a research subject, nothing more. You understand? If we let ourselves become emotionally compromised on this, it will ruin the work. He is Patient H7. You are Nurse Rucker. I am your boss! End of discussion!" he said with adamance.

Nurse Rucker pulled him in and kissed his cheek. "Yes, of course, doctor. Professional integrity, always," she coolly said as she walked back toward the Observation Room.

Killiecrankie blushed, looking around and making sure no one saw, then made his way back down the hall, as well.

A few long moments later, the door to one of the unused office spaces opened.

Inside, Phillip Killiecrankie, Jr., Phillip Sr.'s oldest son and lead medical personnel for the sanatorium, stood with a violent expression on his face. He had come down the corridor from another patient's room when he heard the commotion between Patient H7 and Lt. Col. Braxton. Being the one who alerted the Lt. Col. to come down to Kentucky and knowing the fallout he would have to endure from his father because of that, he hid in the unused office rather than be seen by them both, and, subsequently, overheard everything that had occurred.

The revelation of his father and Nurse Rucker and the product of Patient H7 from that arrangement made him feel anger, rage, and blatant betrayal. Phillip Jr. clenched his fists into balls of hate, seething with passionate rage, but composed himself before heading off in the opposite direction.

He followed the corridor to an office marked "Morrison Killiecrankie, M.D." and immediately walked inside.

In the corner, near an open filing cabinet, stood a very tall, very thin man wearing a doctor's jacket and reading a file. He turned to see Phillip Jr. standing in the doorway, clearly agitated by something.

"Hey, big brother. How's it going? You seem very distressed," Morrison observed.

"That's an understatement, Morris." Phillip Jr. glanced back out into the hallway, making sure no one was there, and then turned back to his brother, "We've got a really big problem on our hands."

Morrison immediately recognized the serious nature in Phillip Jr.'s voice. He placed the file back and, closed the cabinet, then asked, "What can I do to help, big brother?"

Phillip Jr., with dark intentions behind his voice, asked, "Do you have your leather strap handy?"

Chapter Three
"The Secrets of the Asylum"

East Henderson County
July 21, 1986 | 11:48 A.M.

Special Agent Whittaker spent the rest of the morning familiarizing himself with the thick case file of disappearances that had plagued Henderson County for the past three decades. By his count, more than thirty official disappearances had occurred in the county dating from the Summer of 1955 to the Spring of 1986.

Of those thirty, at least half had been discovered deceased, and, of those found dead, six had been subjected to horrific, torturous murders. The manner of death in which former Colonel Will Braxton had been discovered in his home in Fredericksburg was also noted as the cause of death of several missing people in the Henderson County Sheriff's case log.

Another cause of death attributed to a couple of the missing person cases appeared to be from a highly deadly, pressurized pathogen called Tormerdol. Originally engineered by the US Military during the Vietnam War, it had been used by military personnel in hostile areas as an effective way to clear heavy fighting zones to help US troops mobilize attacks behind enemy lines. However, its use was banned when it was discovered that when elevated levels of the pathogen were introduced into dense populations, its effects were astronomically fatal, not only eliminating human life but vegetation, as well.

It had also been discovered that personnel working deep undercover for the CIA were decimating hundreds of villages spanning the entire southern border of Southeast Asia by overexposure to the chemical during unsanctioned military operations.

Thousands of innocent people suffered from internal chemical burns due to an overabundance of the pathogen, which led to their airways turning to liquefied ash. They literally burned to death from the inside. It was a horrible way for people to die, resulting in hundreds of mass graves that would eventually be covered up by the Military Industrial Complex. How could such a volatile weapon banned from military use be found on a Medical Examiner's autopsy report in Henderson, Kentucky? Unfortunately, the autopsy can only determine the cause of death, not the motive of death.

After hours of reading case file after case file, SA Whittaker leaned back in his seat and closed his eyes. He was picturing each victim in each disappearance case, recounting the details he had just read, trying to piece together the final moments for each victim.

During his time at the bureau, he developed an interesting approach to casework when dealing with murder victims. He called it the "Ten Minute Window." Whittaker had become fascinated with what victims had possibly experienced in the final ten minutes of their lives. He theorized that the majority of a case on any one victim could be fully explained if you were able to piece together what happened in the final ten minutes of that person's life.

Who were they with?

What did they say?

What sounds did they hear?

Where were they going?

What were they doing?

Did they anticipate their death?

On the surface, it seems simplistic and obvious, but for Whittaker, that vital "Ten Minute Window" always provided the first domino that would fall in a set of questions that would ultimately explain a homicide in its entirety. All of this would be corroborated by any suspect he would interrogate using his unorthodox approach to questioning a suspect. Thus, the moniker of "The Philosopher" was dubbed upon him.

As Whittaker sat in the chair, eyes closed, picturing the case file victims, his thoughts began to drift as if falling off a cliff into a deep chasm. The visuals in his mind formed into a dark, swirling vortex, and in a quick moment, his brain went completely quiet.

He stood there, in his mind, staring at the dark nothingness, when in the distance, a rumbling sound slowly quaked toward him. Slow at first and then faster. Faster. So much faster! When, suddenly, out of the void, a voice called out loud and clear, breaking the barriers between reality and imagination...

"ASYLUM!!"

Whittaker lurched forward in his seat, gasping for air and rubbing both sides of his head. A massive headache had formed, almost instantaneously, and, as quickly as it came, it vanished, returning him to normal.

He took fast breaths and regained his composure as he heard footsteps approaching and voices talking out in the hall.

Sheriff Dobson and his deputies reentered the small briefing room and sat down with SA Whittaker.

"You've had a chance to go over the case files, Whittaker. What do you think?" asked Sheriff Dobson.

"You *definitely* have a serial killer on your hands." he bluntly responded."

Dobson took a breath in a way that said "I was hoping you wouldn't say that."

"Out of the many disappearances your county has logged, I have been able to make a connection between six of the deceased victims that were recovered to the redacted files on Dr. Killiecrankie and his sanatorium," Whittaker conveyed as he passed around photos of the victims in question.

He continued, "Each one of these victims was related to employees that used to work for the sanatorium. And in each case, the victims appeared to have been pushed to a point of complete breakdown. No different than when torture is used as a form of interrogation to obtain information. Only, I don't know that our suspect ever got the answers they were looking for, considering the number of disappearances and deaths. Some of the missing persons' deaths have no visible connection to the others, but the brutality of their deaths makes me believe they're all connected. There's clearly a methodology, though they tried to not make the pattern so obvious. Each victim was taken at the right time as to not draw too much suspicion to their disappearance, and, by the time their body is discovered, it appears as a random death. The only exception is the condition of the body and the method of murder for the six connected to Dr. Killiecrankie. Being beaten to death by a leather strap certainly raises red flags for me considering my case back home. But I have to be honest, the deaths involving Tormerdol have me more concerned. We're talking about the possibility of chemical genocide if this person feels so inclined."

Sheriff Dobson quickly perked up, "How can you be so sure that Tormerdol would be a viable threat to this community? The ME's autopsy reports showed only trace amounts on two victims and nothing about the reports was conclusive with regard to foul play."

"I've studied thousands of pages of medical reports and military war records on the pathogen dating back to Vietnam. The only reason you found trace amounts is because the bodies hadn't sat long enough for the pathogen to completely dissipate from the lungs and internal tissue. Tormerdol works off blood cells and oxygen. It's introduced through the airways via oxygen intake, then begins to seek out and attack active blood cells. Once it begins its attack, it doesn't stop. The heart cannot keep up with the massive amount of blood loss, and the pathogen begins to eat through the internal tissues of the body until there's nothing else. Once viable oxygen and blood cells are destroyed, the pathogen dissipates and dies. The trace amounts your Medical Examiner found on those two victims were from bodies discovered within the first twenty-four hours of disappearance. All the other victims that were missing person cases that were found to have died from some extreme viral sickness or odd internal injuries were misdiagnosed on the autopsy. If you were to exhume those two bodies with trace amounts of Tormerdol, I guarantee the autopsy would find no traces present and the cause of death would be misdiagnosed as natural causes or something stupid like Tuberculosis. Trust me, Tormerdol was used a number of times here," said Whittaker.

"But that's a military-grade, weaponized pathogen that was banned in the '70s. How would someone even find that these days?" posited Sheriff Dobson.

"I have contacts in the military that might be able to help. If we can figure that out, we'll certainly be on the heels of whoever is responsible for a helluva lot of dead people," said Whittaker.

"So we've got a serial killer who likes to beat people to death, burn people's lungs and throats from the inside, and also likes to kidnap random crazy people all along the East Coast. That's just great." snarked Deputy Martin.

"There's a connective thread between all the missing and dead people here in Henderson County to all the missing mental health facility patients between here and Washington.

What that connection is and why it's happening is the key to solving the mystery of all of this. As I alluded to earlier, if we use what we know from the Colonel Braxton crime scene, we can deduce that one person is committing these murders with a large number of accomplices. How many accomplices? I can't be for sure, but the high number of missing patients is a harrowing indicator of the *possible* number," Whittaker said with an ominous tone.

"I am certain about one thing, though. Whoever this person is, he has an agenda in mind, and he is chomping at the bit to show someone, anyone, and everyone what it is he has to say."

Sheriff Dobson and his deputies sat in silence, processing what Whittaker was laying out for them.

After a few moments, Deputy Harkins asked, "Any ideas where to start, Special Agent Whittaker?"

"I do. From what I read in the files here and the information I had already collected before coming here to Henderson, I learned that Dr. Killiecrankie was discovered murdered inside the Western Kentucky Rehabilitation and Sanatorium in 1963, correct?" he asked.

"Correct," replied Sheriff Dobson.

"Oh, Christ, just call it what it is. The loony bin!" quipped Deputy Martin. "Or at least just say 'asylum' instead of all that other stuff, no one calls it Western Kentucky blah blah blah anymore."

The word "*Asylum*" echoed slightly in SA Whittaker's head. The dark void in his mind began to appear again. This wasn't the first time in his life this sensation had happened to him, but it certainly was the most impactful and most impressionable occurrence.

He took two quick, deep breaths and continued. "Fine... asylum, loony bin, whatever. He was found dead in early '63 under some odd circumstances, and the asylum was permanently shut down, correct?"

Dobson shot a glance at Martin, who wasn't making eye contact, before halfway nodding in agreement to Whittaker.

"And I believe from what I have read he also had a couple of children that worked with him at the asylum. Two boys? They left and started their own practices here in the city in mid to late 1962. Do we know if those two men are still around?"

"Sure they are. Phillip Jr. and Morrison Killiecrankie. They have private practices here in town, and they also run the mental health department at Tranquil Meadows Health over on Sand Lane. Good doctors, nice fellas," replied Deputy Harkins.

"Well, since you seem to like them, I think you would be perfect to go to the 'Doctor Brothers' and inform them of my investigation. I would like to have a sit down with them and ask some questions about their time and association with the asylum and their father," he instructed the young deputy.

Whittaker then turned to Dobson and Martin and said, "As for us, I have a bit of a field trip in mind, if you gentlemen will indulge me."

"I don't like the sound of that," Deputy Martin muttered.

"You want to see the asylum, don't you?" Sheriff Dobson

asked, already knowing the answer.

"Has anyone ever told you that you're very perceptive?" Whittaker asked with a smile.

Sheriff Dobson returned the smile, and everyone stood up to go to their assignments.

Standing outside on the sidewalk, Whittaker watched as Deputy Harkins started up his cruiser and headed out to speak to the Killiecrankie brothers. With any luck, by the end of the day, the doctors would be able to fill in some history for Whittaker about their father and their positions within the now-vacant facility.

Old news articles that had been added to the expanded police file concerning the asylum and Dr. Killiecrankie, Sr. had shown the complete surprise of the death of their father by the sons and their personal vow to try and honor his legacy in the area through their medical practices.

By all accounts, it was a tragedy that had lasting effects on the Killiecrankie family. However, circumstances surrounding the death of Dr. Phillip Killiecrankie, Sr. had brought up quite a few questions inside the active brain of Whittaker, and he was hoping the drive out to the abandoned asylum would give him time to have those questions answered by Sheriff Dobson.

Dobson and Martin pulled up to the sidewalk in the sheriff's car and Whittaker immediately hopped in the back seat. Within minutes, the trio were heading east out of town on Highway 60, windows halfway down with a wave of thick, heated summer air rushing throughout the interior.

Whittaker leaned forward and struck up a conversation.

"So, Sheriff, I have several questions about the circumstances of Dr. Killiecrankie's death. Something isn't adding up, and I noticed from the old reports that you were a newly sworn-in deputy at the time. I thought maybe you could shed some light on the subject."

"What's your concern, SA Whittaker," the sheriff responded as he kept his eyes forward.

"Well, for starters, the reports say he was discovered beaten to death in one of the rooms known to house violent patients, yet none of those violent patients were in the room with the deceased doctor."

Sheriff Dobson didn't respond.

"And the autopsy report says he had been beaten to death at least four months prior to the discovery of the body?"

Dobson remained facing forward.

"I guess my question is, how does the death of a doctor in his *own* facility go unnoticed for four months without anyone raising any questions about his being missing? He has two sons who worked for him for years, they bow out of the asylum the year prior, and now seven months later, he's discovered beaten to death in a fully-funded, operational asylum with no witnesses and no reports of a missing person. None of this makes sense, sheriff."

Deputy Martin had been staring out the window on the drive, but as Whittaker spoke, he turned and gave his full attention, looking at the sheriff.

Based on his eyes, even he conceded that what was on record made zero sense.

Sheriff Dobson mildly shifted in his seat, then spoke, "Truth be told, SA Whittaker, by the time the '60s rolled around, the public had lost faith in the doctor, or lost a need for the facility, or plainly just lost interest in the Sanatorium altogether. I think it would be fair to say that the sons had also lost faith in their father's ability to run the facility properly. There was some bad blood there, I think. You have to understand what it's like in a small town in a rural area like this. When people make up their minds about you, that's just how it is. Fair or not fair, that's just the reality. Dr. Killiecrankie had such a bad reputation with people around here that, eventually, everyone stopped paying attention to what he was doing out there. They stopped caring."

Dobson glanced in the mirror and could see that Whittaker wasn't finished talking on the subject.

Deputy Martin pointed up ahead and said, "The turn is coming up, Sheriff."

Dobson signaled and made the slow turn onto the beat-up, gravel road with thick grass-patches taking over the center of the lane. Along the drive, large oaks and maples hovered overhead creating an eerie canopy that looked as if they would swallow the car whole at any moment.

Within moments, the highway disappeared behind the car, and all that was left to see was the dense, surrounding forest.

After nearly a mile, the tree line widened and a massively overgrown field sprawled out several hundred yards, centered perfectly in front of a very large, condemned-looking building.

The lane faded out to the right and the gravel disappeared completely, leaving only overgrown grass where a laneway used to be that circled in front of the building. Dilapidated stone steps led up to a doorway that once had a set of double doors, but those had been either rotted away by time or destroyed by vandals. The opening that was left revealed a dark, ominous interior, that Whittaker stared at intensely. The opening was very reminiscent of the visual he had previously experienced back in the small meeting room at the Sheriff's Office.

The word "*Asylum*" echoed in his head again as the car came to a complete stop.

All three men stepped out of the vehicle and began taking stock of the sorry state of the land and the building.

In almost every direction, a thick combination of oaks and maples surrounded the property, creating a beautiful representation of country life in Kentucky. Their leaves full of green color and life dancing in the warm summer breeze created a brief sense of peace within Whittaker, but that quickly went away as he surveyed the rest of the property.

The grounds had not been cared for in decades.

Windows were either shattered completely or boarded up. All the decorative stone of the surrounding walls and partition walls in the courtyard had been picked apart by thieves looking to resale intact blocks for a quick buck. From the ground, the men could see that many sections of the old roof were sagging, caved in, or flat-out missing.

Time had not been kind to this old building.

"Well, here ya are. Home sweet home," Deputy Martin chuckled to himself.

Even Whittaker had to laugh, as well. "Definitely seen better days, for sure."

"So, what are you hoping to gain from coming out here, Special Agent Whittaker?" Asked Dobson as he carefully scaled the steps to the entrance.

The other men followed.

"I think there's more to the story of this old place than you're letting on if I'm being perfectly honest. Any and all stories relating to this building and Dr. Killiecrankie have some shrouded mystery hanging over them, and no one seems to want to shoot straight on it. Even you," said Whittaker as he pointed toward Dobson.

The sheriff didn't respond, though Whittaker could sense that he felt mildly offended by the statement.

They were now standing in what used to be a beautiful, large foyer. Spray-painted graffiti lined many of the interior walls with dirt and debris covering the other parts of the walls and floor. The building felt unsafe the moment they stepped in, but Whittaker was determined to follow through on the urging of the voice of the void.

Dobson led the other two men through the broken down, debris-filled corridors, cutting through open rooms and working their way around sections of hallways that were blocked by stacks of old furniture, patient beds, and abandoned medical instruments.

After making their way through a dimly lit set of offices, they found themselves in a narrow corridor lined with rooms that had observation windows. On the left, a room once marked "Observation Room 2" was barely legible on the door, and the interior was visibly damaged with massive chunks of the wall missing and a large crack in the ceiling in the far corner.

The observation window had a noticeably long crack at the base, above the frame, and a murky substance resembling thick, dried-up blood or caked-up mud stretched across the floor from the near wall to the middle of the room and back toward the doorway. The window on the opposite side of the doorway was destroyed with glass shard remnants scattered about on the floor in the hallway.

"Something came through this window at a very rapid pace," Whittaker commented as he observed the scene through a forensic eye.

Sheriff Dobson nodded in agreement.

Two doorways were down on the right. The door frame missing its door revealed a large open room with the remaining frames of four twin-sized beds that circled the outer perimeter of the room. In the center of the room were two activity tables that sat roughly six feet apart from each other, and, in the space between the two tables, a rather large, anamorphic outline of a dark stain rested prominently on display on the floor.

Sheriff Dobson stepped close to it, paused, then turned to Whittaker and said, "The final resting place for Dr. Phillip

Killiecrankie, Sr."

Whittaker stepped forward and stood next to Sheriff Dobson, staring at the dark stain on the floor which was the final dregs of blood that flowed from the doctor. Whittaker could not shake the feeling of being left completely in the dark about vital details concerning the discovery of Dr. Killiecrankie's death in 1963. Dobson had been rather standoffish when the subject was brought forth, but now he had no choice but to discuss the matter. Whittaker was going to make sure of that.

"You've been ducking the issue of Killiecrankie every opportunity you can when I broach the subject, and I'm not going to let you keep being coy about what happened here. There, is something that isn't in that file, and I want to know what it is, Sheriff," Whittaker said in a very demanding tone.

"I take offense to your tone, Special Agent Whittaker. I assure you I have no idea what you're talking about. We were called out here one day in '63 for a loud disturbance. When we got out here, we found the doctor dead. That's all," replied Sheriff Dobson.

The tone of his voice was not convincing.

From a small corner in the back of Special Agent Whittaker's mind, a low voice softly echoed from the void,

"He's lying..."

Without thinking, Whittaker blurted out, "You're lying!"

Dobson and Martin both turned to Whittaker with surprised looks on their faces.

Whittaker took a step back, covering his mouth, embarrassed at his outburst. At that moment, he felt like he wasn't in control of his own body, as if he was being controlled by a puppeteer.

Whittaker stood silent, not saying a word.

"I am not lying to you, Whittaker," said Sheriff Dobson, almost as if he was trying to convince himself of what he was saying. He stepped toward Whittaker with a concerned look on his face. As he did, the expression on Whittaker's face shifted, and it caught the experienced lawman off guard.

"SANATORIUM SHUT DOWN! PATIENTS MISSING! STAFF MISSING! COVER UP!"

The words flowed from Whittaker's mouth in an uncontrollable wave of assertions. He had no control over what was happening to him, and the voice inside his mind wouldn't let up.

More words flowed out of the dark chasm in his mind, and the pace was too much to keep up with. Whittaker stumbled backward against one of the tables in the center of the room with Dobson and Martin looking on at a loss as to what was going on or what to do.

Whittaker grabbed the sides of his head, fighting a battle against a shapeless entity inside his mind. The void inside felt as if it was trying to envelop him from within, but Whittaker pushed back in his mind and screamed,

"NO!"

The void evaporated into a fine mist and vanished.

The force of the cerebral encounter had slammed Whittaker to the ground, and, within seconds, the loudness in his head became quiet and the pain quickly went away. He lay on the ground for a few seconds, catching his breath.

Dobson and Martin stood over him in complete disbelief at what they just witnessed.

"What the hell was that?!" yelled Martin.

"Are you okay, Whittaker?" asked Dobson.

The special agent made his way back to his feet, shaking the proverbial cobwebs from his head and dusting off his suit. After pulling himself back together, he looked at Dobson and said, "I think you have some more information you're not sharing with me."

Dobson smirked, "I think the same could be said about you."

As the two men stared at each other in an apparent stalemate, from across the hall, behind a closed door, the sound of shuffling feet echoed out loudly and all three men immediately turned and drew their weapons. Without saying a word, they took tactical positioning to the door, with Whittaker taking the lead.

Martin took position on the left side of the closed door, while Dobson followed closely behind Whittaker to the right, watching his back and keeping a check on Martin's back in the other direction.

The professionalism was impressive.

After signaling a count and getting confirmation from the other two, Whittaker took a step back and kicked the aged, dry-rotted door to oblivion, sending wood shrapnel flying in all directions. All three men took position in the doorway to assess the threat from the office.

Inside, two young kids huddled close to each other on the floor in the far corner, refusing to look up at their attackers.

Sheriff Dobson pulled back his firearm and let out an aggravated huff.

"SAM AND MICAH DAVIS!! Get yer asses over here right now!"

The boys instantly recognized the Sheriff's voice and quickly made their way over to the three officers.

Dobson was not pleased. "I have told you I don't know how many times that you are not allowed on this property, you understand?!"

The boys never looked up and just quietly responded with, "Yes, sir."

"Next time I catch you two sneaking around here, I'm gonna write your daddy a ticket for trespassing and let him deal with you two when he gets home!"

Their eyes grew as big as saucers.

"Now get yer butts home, and do not touch anything on your way out of here, God Bless."

The boys quickly scurried off as Dobson and Martin took turns venting their frustrations over the hellion kids they had come to know very well the past few years.

As the sheriff and his deputy spoke, Special Agent Whittaker turned his attention down the hall away from the entrance from which they had come. A soft ringing sound began to filter through his mind. The void inside began to appear but not as aggressive as before.

Calming. Beckoning.

"Follow the hallway. Office at the end on the right."

Whittaker didn't question it or pause for caution or fear. He was being shown the way. To what? He could not fathom, or speculate but something was definitely guiding him and he could not turn away from it.

He headed down the hallway, leaving Dobson and Martin who almost didn't notice him walking away. They quickly caught up with him and questioned what he was up to.

"Where you going, Whittaker? There's nothing down this hallway but more offices," explained Dobson.

Whittaker didn't respond and kept walking. The three men made their way to the office at the end of the hallway on the right. The door was missing, and Whittaker immediately stepped in.

Inside were remnants of what used to be an office years ago with broken furniture and file folders missing their contents scattered about on the floor. Straight across from the door was another door-less opening that led into a short hallway.

"Go straight"

Whittaker continued, taking his cues from the directions coming from an unknown source within.

The room beyond the hallway was a maintenance room lined with old implements, tools, and various items commonly found in a workshop. At the back of the room was a giant steel door recessed into the wall. On the ceiling and the floor, matching quarter circle tracks were rusted out with large pieces of plaster dangling from a frame barely hanging on to the roller mechanism stuck in the track.

"False Wall."

Whittaker pulled the steel door which surprisingly opened with ease. It led to a set of steel stairs that went down a flight and a half and opened up into a small corridor. At the end of the corridor, he opened the closed door and came face-to-face with an entire section of the asylum that was never meant to be known to the public.

It was windowless and dark, and it took a few moments for their eyes to adjust.

Dobson removed a flashlight from his belt and shined the light around in various directions. Whittaker looked around, completely surprised by the finding, but when he turned to Dobson and Martin, he was taken aback at how the two local lawmen seemed to already know about this secret.

He stepped forward to question them about the additional portion of the asylum when his mysterious guiding voice stopped him.

"Left down the corridor. Library on the left. Behind the wood panel of the bookshelf."

Whittaker took off running, with Dobson and Martin in full sprint behind him, confused but intrigued by their new acquaintance.

He found the library halfway down the corridor. It was an absolute mess. Furniture had been overturned and savagely broken. Books were thrown about and many holes had been smashed through the walls. Every piece of furniture had been destroyed except for a small table and one bookshelf built into the near wall to the right.

Whittaker walked toward it, inspecting the empty bookshelves one-be-one, looking for a weak spot in the panel to the back. It was a rather easy search and within seconds, Whittaker had the panel completely ripped away from the wall, exposing a small void. Dead center sat a wooden box about the size of a hat box from the 1950s.

Dobson and Martin looked on in disbelief.

"How the hell did you know that was there?" asked Sheriff

Dobson.

Martin was so stunned he couldn't speak.

The guiding voice from the void had gone stone-cold quiet now. It had guided him where he needed to be.

"If I tried to explain how I was able to find this, you would probably lock me up in a place like this and throw away the key. It's completely unbelievable. Martin, help me with this table, please," he said, motioning to the deputy who was still stunned but obliged him all the same.

Martin assisted Whittaker in flipping over the small table to place the wooden box on and examine its contents.

Dobson observed quietly, but then spoke, "There's something not right about any of this, Whittaker. You owe me an explanation."

"I owe you an explanation? You're the one clearly holding out important details about a lot of different aspects of this case. Something is preventing you from being completely forthright with me, and it's bugging the hell out of me. But I tell you what, the second you feel like offering up some of what you're hiding, then I'll be more than happy to share with the class, as well, deal? Until that time, let's focus on what this is," he snapped back, turning away from the sheriff and refocusing on the wooden box from behind the bookshelf.

Whittaker took a deep breath, and then slowly opened the box.

Inside, there was a stack of pristine file folders carefully wrapped with a protective cover and neatly placed inside the box. On top of the stack, a small, sealed envelope with very dignified and professional penmanship was written,

"To whoever may find this box, this is my life's work..."

They each took glances at each other, trying to ascertain who should do the honors.

Dobson nodded to Whittaker who then removed a small penknife from his pocket and carefully cut open the envelope.

Inside, a single folded piece of notepad paper with the letterhead reading

"From the Office Archives of Dr. Phillip Artemis Killiecrankie, Sr., PhD.".

The letter was very short, and straight to the point.
It read:

"If you are reading this note, then I have fallen victim to villainy perpetrated by my sons, Phillip, Jr. and Morrison Killiecrankie. They are responsible for my death, the imprisonment of Nurse Abigail Rucker, and the repeated abuse and torment of patients who are under my care. Please, hold them accountable for their crimes and bring them to justice. These files must be taken to Lt. Col. Braxton in Washington, D.C. immediately so that the United States Military can continue my research. The next steps of evolution depend upon it!

- Dr. Phillip Killiecrankie"

Dobson, Martin, and Whittaker all stood in silence after reading the note. If true, this changed the entire complexity of the investigation and put a giant bullseye directly on the backs of the Killiecrankie brothers.

Sheriff Dobson took a small step back and looked at Whittaker, who was now opening files from the box.

"What is the likelihood of this being remotely true?" Dobson asked out of shock and curiosity.

"A very high percentage considering the signature on the note is a spot-on match for the signature in these files. I'd have to confirm with files we have back at the bureau but, I'm leaning toward very likely," said Whittaker.

Deputy Martin was just as stunned as the other two, but his shock turned to focus as he helped Whittaker thumb through the folders.

"These files... they're... they're all the same patient. Every one of them," stammered Martin as he opened file after file. "Patient H7-1... Patient H7-2... It's gotta be the same patient, right? What do the numbers mean?"

"Experiments!!"

Out of the void, the voice returned, sending Whittaker reeling back from the table. A low-frequency hum steadied itself in his brain, racing down into his ears and vanishing as quickly as it formed.

After the hum subsided, a realization hit Whittaker.

He darted to the table, and skipped down to the last file. It read, "Patient I7-1." The folder had one page of information and nothing else. Whittaker placed it back in the box and grabbed the next folder. Stamped on the front was "Patient H7-31." He quickly opened the folder and scanned the information.

Part of the way down, one line stood out to the special agent.

"Subject - Aged 7 years - Has severely regressed in abilities since last treatment."

Whittaker held the file up to show Dobson and Martin. "This number right here... 31... that's how many times he was experimented on. Seven years old! Look at the date!" he exclaimed in disbelief as he held the file closer to Dobson's face. "September 17th, 1962!"

Both the sheriff and the deputy were speechless.

Whittaker huffed and turned back to the wooden box, re-stacking all the files back into the box, picking it up, and then heading out of the room.

Dobson and Martin followed.

Whittaker was nearly running, fuming in anger, disbelief, shock, and confusion. Something deep within him had directed him to find these files. Something from way down inside his very being was showing him a path that he wasn't sure he should follow but was compelled to follow. A calling, one might say. But what did it all mean? How would this all come to an end?

The only way Special Agent Whittaker was going to find his answers was to continue walking the path.

He navigated his way through the catacombs of aged debris and broken medical relics back to the main floor and out the defaced entryway to the Sheriff's car still parked in the overgrown drive.

Whittaker placed the wooden box on the trunk, opened the back door, and retrieved his briefcase. By this point, Dobson and Martin had made their way back to the car, and they had concerns and questions.

"Where is all this leading, Whittaker?" asked Deputy Martin. "You seem to have some ideas of what is going on here, so please, I beg of you, fill us in," implored Dobson.

Whittaker opened his briefcase and pulled out the evidence bag containing a single file page with a large bloody handprint. "Remember this? This was stuck to the bloody back of Colonel Braxton. We have a handwritten letter saying these files needed to go to him in the event of Killiecrankie's death. Why?"

Dobson and Martin had no answer.

Whittaker continued, "Look at the patient's name... H7-423. Four-hundred and twenty-three experiments! Phillip, Sr. died in 1962. There's no way in hell he performed almost four hundred more experiments on this seven-year-old kid in a couple of months. Look here... no date! Just a note that says, 'Final Treatment.' It's signed by Phillip, Jr."

Dobson's face went flush and Martin just stood still, covering his mouth with his hands.

The truth about the facility was starting to emerge, but Whittaker's focus was on his next move. He moved in close to Sheriff Dobson and in a low, calm voice he said, "You are going to tell me everything that you're holding back on, or, so help me God, I will beat it out of you. But right now, we are going to go talk to the brothers because I have a helluva lot of questions that need answering. Do I, *now*, have your full cooperation, Sheriff?"

Dobson let out a long exhale as if he had been carrying a massive weight on his shoulders for a very long time.

"Yes, Special Agent Whittaker. You now have my full cooperation."

The radio in the Sheriff's car crackled and a voice spoke out for him.

"Sheriff Dobson, this is Deputy Harkins, come back."

Dobson grabbed the receiver.

"This is Dobson, go ahead Deputy."

"What's your 20, come back."

"Currently at the abandoned sanatorium out here off 60, over.."

"Is SA Whittaker still with you, come back."

"Affirmative."

"Well, then ya'll need to hurry back here."

"What's the issue, Deputy?"

"Well, sir... you're not going to believe this, but... we just got calls that both the doctors are missing."

Chapter Four
"The Death of Killiecrankie"

Western Kentucky Rehabilitation and Sanatorium
October 19, 1962 | 9:46 A.M.

"Testing, Testing... checking levels and microphone is working... Dr. Phillip Killiecrankie with test subject Patient H7, testing phase number 31, Nineteenth of October, 1962... target of testing phase was to re-engage progress made by Patient H7... subject, aged seven years, has severely regressed in abilities since last treatment... which was three weeks ago... patient has shown rapid decline in overall demeanor and output has registered it's lowest measurable since last summer of 1961... electrode nodules were applied and settings locked in at 35 volts to act as a stimulant to the subject... Nurse Rucker, when you type up this report, I want it to be clear in my notes that this test was merely to re-engage the subject to the progress he's already made, we are not advancing his program at this time, this was only a recovery treatment... During this exam, the subject repeatedly failed to engage in dialog with myself, be it through his telepathy or speaking voice... subject appeared heavily sedated though medications are not a part of his regimen at this time. We'll definitely have to go over his parameters with the rest of the staff to ensure there are no mistakes during the administering of medications... when applying the electrodes, faint bruising was detected on the upper back and shoulders of the subject, and injuries that appeared to be older and almost healed, along with a series of patches of busted blood vessels on the lower back... patient

refused to explain where the injuries came from, my fear is he was mistakenly placed into Patient Room A6 where the older, more aggressive patients are housed... this type of mistake cannot be allowed to happen again for the safety of Patient H7 and the progress of this program... electro-shock treatment resulted in zero change of patient readout, from a scientific standpoint, I cannot explain the patients decline... Patient H7 is back in his room resting comfortably at this time... when you return from your wellness check on Patient I7, we'll hopefully be able to put our heads together and come to a quick and satisfactory resolution and solution for H7's decline... end of report."

Dr. Killiecrankie turned off his recording device and gathered up his files and tapes of the session with Patient H7. It had been an uneventful session and the doctor's confusion and frustrations over his most valuable test subjects' recent decline kept his mind preoccupied and oblivious to his surroundings.

Over the past three weeks, he had thought of nothing but Patient H7 and what different medical methods he could use to reignite the spark that was once a bright and promising flame just one year prior when Lt. Col. Braxton came for results.

In early September, Braxton came calling again to see if the doctor's brightest prospect had made any more advancements, and he had, by leaps and bounds. He was having full conversations with Killiecrankie and Nurse Rucker via telepathy, and before Lt. Col. Braxton had even stepped foot out of his Lincoln Continental when it arrived, Patient H7 had already greeted him in his head.

The young patient and the Lt. Col. had a full conversation

before Braxton had even made it to the Observation Room. Braxton had been highly impressed. So much, in fact, that he was willing to give another extension to Dr. Killiecrankie in the hopes that the program would be able to find a way to replicate his findings and come up with a serum that was reverse-engineered from the blood properties of Patient H7 that could then be used to create highly advanced operatives with special unlocked abilities based off their DNA code.

It was a very exciting time for the doctor and his quest for biological and evolutionary advancement until the rapid decline of Patient H7 brought everything to a massive halt.

With files in hand, Dr. Killiecrankie made his way through the corridors from Test Room C to the main offices at the front of the facility. He stepped into Nurse Rucker's office to hand off the files, fully expecting to see his confidant back from her trip, sitting at her desk, filing reports, and getting caught up on her paperwork.

The room was empty, and her desk was a chaotic mess of piled-up file folders.

At first, he found it odd but didn't give it too much thought. He had recently sent her off with an assistant to do a quarterly follow-up on a patient who had spent a short amount of time in the facility in the latter part of 1956. The patient lived in the Northeast portion of the country, and Nurse Rucker would often make this trip by car and would also plan extra personal time during these visits. For her to be gone for an extended period of time was not out of the ordinary.

Killiecrankie, satisfied with his deductions, promptly went

to work cleaning up the files on the desk.

His entire file system was immaculate and was always being updated. Nurse Rucker had implemented the system within the first few years of her employment at the facility, and Dr. Killiecrankie could not have been more pleased with its results. The day-to-day operations were kept in pristine shape and easily accessed at any given point of the day. His more detailed files that required a higher level of discretion were even more organized and stored in secure, locked filing cabinets, in the small room that connected both of their offices.

Taking an hour of his day to file the paperwork that had mounted up on Nurse Rucker's desk, Dr. Killiecrankie stepped into his office and sat at his desk. It had been a few years since he spoke with the family of the patient Nurse Rucker had set off to visit, and her absence had reminded him of that.

As he sat, he opened the bottom drawer of his desk, reaching to the very back and removing a folder that had "Patient 17" stamped on the front. Paper-clipped to the outside of the folder was a small piece of paper with a phone number written in black pen with an area code for New Hampshire.

Killiecrankie picked up the receiver of his desk phone and dialed the number. After several rings, the phone clicked and the deep voice of a man answered on the other end.

"Hello..."

"Good morning, Arthur, it's Dr. Phillip Killiecrankie. Do, you remember me?"

There was commotion on the phone, and then a long

pause before the man replied in a low serious tone."I thought you said you would never contact me directly.?"

"You're right Arthur; our parameters for this arrangement was that you would report the patient's progress through Nurse Rucker and my correspondence would be the same, but I just felt compelled..."

Arthur cut in abruptly. "This is the second time you've called me this week, Phillip. You're breaking your agreement! Look, I know you're paying us very well to continue with this program, but he's more than just a patient to us now, he's our little boy, and if it's all the same, I think I'd rather just keep the interactions with Nurse Rucker. He's taken a fondness to her, and I don't want there to be a chance that he discovers how he came to be our son."

"What do you mean this is the second time I've called? I haven't called you this week. I haven't spoken to you in three years, Arthur... Who called you?"

"It was a man who sounded just like you and said that the situation had changed and that I should come down to Kentucky to discuss the matter at hand. It was very odd, and it unnerved me. I did exactly what you told me when we first started this agreement. You said that if at any point someone calls to meet, even if it's you, to just hang up the phone and get my family away from the house for a few days. And that's what I did. And now you're calling me again."

"But I didn't call you!" Killiecrankie was beside himself. He had not made any calls to anyone outside the state, and no one else on his staff was authorized to make such calls either.

Killiecrankie quickly stood up, pacing back and forth, trying to understand who would pretend to be him. He paused momentarily and glanced down at a newspaper that was folded up and resting on the edge of his desk.

It was a copy of the *Gleaner and Journal,* July 25, 1962, and in this particular edition, sprawled across the front page, was an article detailing the severed business ties of Phillip Killiecrankie, Jr. and Morrison Killiecrankie from their father and his asylum.

Points of interest in the article were the "philosophical differences in approach to medical practice," "hostile working environment," and "unwillingness to evolve with the field of medicine." The article also announced the brothers' grand openings of their individual medical practices, setting up offices in the Henderson City limits, cementing their clean break from their father. His reputation took a massive hit after the article was published, and he kept the copy on his desk as a reminder of his sons' betrayal.

"Arthur, listen to me carefully. You need to move your family!"

"What?! I can't just move my family, what are you talking about?"

"Damnit, listen to me. Something isn't right. You have to move them. You still have the information I gave you for the program, right? The contact in Washington... for the funding?"

"Yes, I still have it...."

"If you do not hear from someone from Washington in the next week, you call that number and you tell them that the program is compromised, you understand? You tell them I said it's compromised, that they need to institute the Disavow Protocol for the program and for *you*."

"Disavow Protocol? What is that?"

"Arthur... I have systems in place to protect you and your family, but you have got to do exactly as I say. Do you understand?"

"I understand."

"Good. When Nurse Rucker returns from her visit with you, I will finalize your son's file and pass that information to my contacts just to be safe."

There was a long pause on the other end of the line.

"What do you mean when she returns? She was never here."

Phillips Killiecrankie's stomach dropped, and a cold chill covered his body.

"No, no... she was there. She was there... she left not too long ago to come up for the quarterly and she should be on her way back now."

"No, Phillip. She was never here. We haven't seen here since the last visit."

Killiecrankie's mind raced and a very dark, foreboding picture was coming into view in his mind, and he did not like the story it was going to tell.

"Arthur, I fear this will be the last time we speak. I'm sorry for any trouble I may have caused you. Please follow my instructions and keep your family safe. Take care."

He hung up the receiver before Arthur could respond.

The clock was ticking.

Dr. Killiecrankie grabbed a small piece of stationary with his letterhead printed across the top and quickly wrote down a note. He then folded it and placed it inside an envelope, sealing it right away. On the outside, he wrote,

"To whomever may find this box, this is my life's work..."

He tucked the letter into his vest pocket and stared at the small piece of paper with Arthur's phone number written on it. Phillip reached back into his desk, found a small matchbook, and removed a single match. Striking it on the phosphorous strip, the small spark ignited the match head into a steady flame. He held the paper to the flame as it quickly caught fire and then turned to ash. He blew out the match and grabbed up the file for Patient I7.

Walking through the small room that connected to Nurse Rucker's office, he stopped at a secured filing cabinet. Using a small key, he unlocked it. The entire front panel opened like a door, revealing another lock, for which he had a second key. He unlocked that one, as well, and emptied the contents of two interior bins.

Very heightened security for these files. Every notation on every experiment, neatly condensed to two separate stacks of file folders, Patient H7 and everyone else, compliments of Nurse Rucker's impressive filing system.

He turned to the other side of the room, opened a cabinet, and searched all the shelves but couldn't find what he was looking for. Frustrated, he stepped out of the room, through Nurse Rucker's office, and out into the main corridor.

Across the hall, a short man in a custodial uniform was pushing a large broom across the floor.

"Hey, Jake, come here for a second," Killiecrankie shouted.

The janitor quickly made his way over.

"Yes, doctor?"

"We should have a roll of protective film or plastic in maintenance. Will you go grab it for me?"

The janitor happily obliged and set off to get the items when Killiecrankie stopped him, "Also... do you happen to remember the last time Nurse Rucker was in?"

The young janitor stood thinking for a quick moment, then said, "I'd say three weeks or so. I'll be right back with that plastic, sir."

Killiecrankie's mind swirled.

He turned and ran back to the small room where he left his files. He grabbed up the stack of files on Patient H7 and quickly read through the last three sessions, checking the dates. Patient H7 had shown a considerable decline in progress during the three weeks that Nurse Rucker had been absent from the facility.

He went back further and checked the sessions that occurred during other times that Nurse Rucker had been gone from the sanatorium. Each time, there was a minimal dip in productive output, but Patient H7 always regained his progress upon her return.

Killiecrankie checked his notes from the session the week that Nurse Rucker recently left, and right there the answer he had overlooked.

"When talking with Patient H7, his demeanor shifted dramatically upon learning that Nurse Rucker was not attending the session. When asked about his relationship to Nurse Rucker, the patient is quoted as saying, "She's my best friend..."

He sat down at the table in the small room and softly laid the file folder on the table.

Killiecrankie had dedicated his life to the pursuit of medical advancement, and those who joined him along the way were his coworkers and associates, nothing more. He had a notoriously off-putting temperament and wasn't known to be a very caring or affectionate man.

This sentiment also applied to his family which, naturally, created an emotional void. He loved his family in only the way that a man who has dedicated his life to his work could love a family: by covering the basic responsibilities required of a husband and father.

The fact that he kept himself emotionally distant from everyone had created a skewed way of approaching his research and this was none more evident than during his time away from Nurse Rucker.

He had desperately kept his emotional impulses in check during his tenure working with the nurse for the simple fact that the two of them together, professionally, garnered a lot of positive strides in the field of medicine, but it could not be denied that their entanglement that produced Patient H7 as an experimental offspring tapped into a side of him that he kept locked away.

From a scientific standpoint, the evidence was conclusive when he looked over the notes for the most recent sessions of Patient H7. Nurse Rucker was a best friend to the patient, but behind the scenes, she was his mother, and that bond was undeniably the key to unlocking all of Patient H7's potential.

Killiecrankie took a deep breath, bolstering his resolve, and immediately knew that he had to find Nurse Rucker, and he hoped that his sons hadn't found her first.

Jake the janitor returned with a large, industrial roll of protective plastic and gave it to the doctor. Killiecrankie used the protective film to wrap around both stacks of files, individually, to preserve their condition.

In the corner, Killiecrankie picked up a small wooden box with a hinged lid and placed the two stacks of files inside. He then removed the letter from his vest pocket and laid it gently onto the stacks of folders and closed the lid.

Between the unsanctioned calls made to Arthur in New Hampshire and Lt. Col. Braxton last summer, Nurse Rucker's disappearance, and the abrupt departure of his sons from the sanatorium that was riddled with inaccuracies, falsehood, and outright fabrications, Phillip Killiecrankie knew that his sons had been planning this for a while. His intuition told him that they had very dark intentions for their father and those associated with him, and if he had any chance of preserving not only himself and his work, he would have to make sure they didn't get their hands on his research.

He quickly made his way down a side corridor, through the backside of the kitchen, into a separate room just off the hallway leading to the receiving dock.

This room was a messy assortment of maintenance and janitorial supplies, tools of all varieties, and a well-stocked shelf of cleaning chemicals.

In the left corner, a large shelf was slightly angled from its normal resting position, revealing a doorway that was left open into a small hallway with a closed door at the end.

Killiecrankie noticed this but didn't pay it particular attention and continued to the opposite corner.

He approached the large, white-painted, wood panel wall with a small handle. He grabbed the handle, and with an easy tug, the wall pulled completely forward and opened out by a recessed track on the floor and ceiling, exposing a large steel door. Killiecrankie opened the door, stepped into the frame, and then pulled the false wall back into position.

He followed the steel steps down from the doorway, following a short hallway to a closed door. He opened the door, and as he entered, flipped a switch on the wall. A completely different, almost brand new in appearance, section of the sanatorium became fully illuminated by the overhead lights.

When construction broke ground on the sanatorium in late 1928, it had been conveniently left out of the news reports that the United States Military had stepped in to offer funding for the project.

Under the guise of savvy real estate dealings and well-invested funds coming off the tail end of the Great Depression, it was easy to create a cover story for the erection of the sanatorium. Some folks suffered financially from the big crash, and then others benefited from the chaos.

That's just how things were back then.

During the construction, Phillip Killiecrankie was very adamant to the men in charge back in Washington that his facility would need an alternate wing located underground in the event that suspicion was ever aroused as to his research and work in the county. With the particulars of their arrangement being of a sensitive nature, the higher-ups agreed, and the extra underground facility was added in the event of "Stealth Emergency Evacuation." Much like the rest of the sanatorium, it was state of the art and cutting edge for its time, but it also could have been chalked up as a waste of time and money.

This section of the facility had only ever been utilized twice in the history of the building, and both of those times were false alarms after mild complaints had been filed with the sheriff's office for patients going beyond the sanatorium grounds onto the property of local residents. On this day, however, Dr. Killiecrankie used the exclusivity and covert placement of the added section to hide his life's work from the motive-driven hands of his sons.

He stepped into the main section of the hallways where three outstretched corridors connected at one focal point, much like tributaries converging on a large river. He turned left, carrying the small wooden box tightly in his hands, following the corridor to a room on the left that was set up like a small den or library with several furnished bookshelves on each of the walls.

During construction, Dr. Killiecrankie had specifically asked that the bookshelf to his right be mounted directly into the frame of the wall, with a void left accessible via a false panel, if he would need to store something of importance during a search of the property.

He left nothing to chance, and only he knew of these small details.

Killiecrankie placed the box on the ground, carefully removed a line of books from the middle shelf, and then lifted the shelf completely out of the casing. Behind where the books stood, he pressed with his palms flat against the panel and lifted straight up. The panel was removed with ease, revealing a rectangular void. The small void measured about eighteen inches wide and no more than twenty-four inches tall, but it was open enough and deep enough for the small wooden box to fit comfortably.

Killiecrankie placed the box inside the void, replaced the panel, the shelf, and the books, and quickly made his way back to the corridor that led up to the main floor. Having confidently hidden his work, he now turned his attention to locating Nurse Rucker.

At the convergence of hallways, he turned to go back upstairs but stopped when he heard a faint sound akin to feet shuffling on the tile floor from the center hallway directly behind him. He turned and paused, wondering if he should investigate.

The noise happened again.

Curiosity overtook him and he started down the corridor. As he followed the noise, he couldn't help but notice that this space, which he had only ever used a handful of times, had the feel and appearance of a space that had been used many times. And recently used, as well.

A large laboratory space on the left-hand side of the hall had its door open and inside, lying on the counter was a notebook with detailed mathematical equations, chemical combinations, and research notes detailing multiple trials of a synthesized pathogen. The elemental configurations were intricate and completely new to the doctor. At the top of one of the pages, in familiar handwriting, it read:

"Possible name for new pathogen: Tormerdol"

Dr. Killiecrankie stepped away from the counter, unaware of what he was looking at, for he never signed off on new chemical manipulation or pathogen testing.

This laboratory was always meant to be a fall-back laboratory in the event of lock-down, it was never supposed to be used concurrently with the upstairs laboratory. His sons had been doing way more than he originally thought, and he became very aware of the grave situation before him, and a wave of fear and uncertainty flushed his inner being.

The sound of shuffling echoed again, much closer this time.

He continued down the hallway, cautiously checking to make sure no one would get the jump on him. Two doors down on the right, diagonally from the laboratory, a room with an open door and no interior light emanating the continuous sound.

Phillip stood next to the doorway, slowly reaching inside and flipping the light switch. He peeked inside, methodically, assessing the situation with no real plan beyond turning the lights on.

On the floor inside, Nurse Rucker lay on the floor, blindfolded, gagged, arms and legs bound by rope, writhing in pain. The rope had cut into her wrists and ankles and fresh blood trickled out over dried, flaking blood on her skin. She was malnourished from starvation, and her once beautiful face bore fresh cuts and bruises.

Killiecrankie rushed to free her from her bindings. As he attempted to remove the blindfold, she screamed and kicked, assuming it was her assailants, with the sound completely muffled by the gag. He was finally able to remove the blindfold, and when their eyes met, a sense of calm washed over her for a brief second as tears began to roll down her face. For the first time in Dr. Killiecrankie's life, he felt something inside that resembled passion that didn't come from a medical discovery.

He quickly removed the gag, and as he did, Nurse Rucker quickly spoke.

"Phillip, you have to go get help! They're here now, you understand, they're here now!!"

Their professional relationship had blurred the lines several times over the years into more personal areas, but they always remained neutral on how they handled the overall connections. This high level of intimacy, professional or otherwise, had created an unspoken language that the two of them were able to connect through. Call it telepathy or just simple human emotion, Killiecrankie knew at that moment that she intended to protect the integrity of what they both had built together. Sending him away would put her at risk, but at least he would have the chance to salvage the situation.

Killiecrankie didn't speak. He didn't freeze. He just reacted.

Turning away, he left her bound on the floor, running in a dead sprint back down the corridor to the stairway leading back to the main floor. As he entered the short hallway leading to the steel steps that would take him to the hidden steel door, the fateful hand of reality reached out and instantly choked the life of hope from the doctor.

Standing at the base of the steel steps, with the hidden steel door leading to salvation atop the stairs behind them, were Phillip, Jr. and Morrison Killiecrankie.

Morrison had a leather strap dangling in his hand while the oldest son held a revolver that was pointed directly at the patriarch of the Killiecrankie family. Phillip, Sr.'s knees went weak, and he knew at that moment, it was the beginning of the end.

"Hello, Father. I see you found your mistress," Phillip, Jr. said with a sly grin.

"Boys, whatever it is you have going on here-"

Morrison cut him off. "Just stop it, Father, it's too late for you..."

"It's not too late to undo this, son," pleaded the doctor.

Phillip, Jr. was already bored with the situation and motioned with the gun in his hand to his dad, "Close the door behind you and follow us..."

As the eldest Killiecrankie closed the door to the secret expansion of the sanatorium, sobbing cries of "NO!" echoed through the corridors beyond and then fell silent as the door closed completely. Killiecrankie complied with his sons, who were clearly in control of the situation at this point, and all three made their way back up to the main floor.

As they stepped beyond the steel door back into the maintenance area, a very broad-shouldered man wearing a dingy maintenance uniform stood ominously in the center of the room staring at the older doctor. He had a prominent scar that ran from the back of his skull, across the top of the head, stopping at the hairline just above his forehead. A name tag stitched to the front of his uniform read "Augy."

He didn't speak, but his heavy breathing could be heard from the next room.

Dr. Killiecrankie stared right back at him briefly and then said, "Ahh, of course. My other son, the mute, is here to see me off as well."

Morrison, with strap in hand, hauled off and landed the leather weapon across the face of his father, sending him crashing to the floor in a heap.

"You lost your right to refer to *my* brother as *your* son," Morrison spouted to his father.

Auguste Killiecrankie was born in 1928 just before ground broke on the sanatorium. As a toddler, a horrific accident occurred during the construction that resulted in a severe head injury and subsequent brain injury. As talented a surgeon Dr. Killiecrankie was, at the time, he wasn't able to fully heal his injured son. He performed several surgeries on the boy over the next few years, and, eventually, Auguste would regain full control of his body except his voice.

After the incident and many surgeries, Auguste became non-verbal. Because of this condition and the hectic schedule of his father, Auguste wasn't mentally healthy enough to learn from his father at the same pace as his older brothers. Where they excelled, he became deficient. The brothers, however, loved him all the same, and from the beginning, they called him Augy. They swore to protect their little brother. Unfortunately for them, their father had other ideas for how to handle his son who he viewed as "less than" or as "broken parts."

Phillip Killiecrankie never acknowledged Augy as his son and instructed the other sons to never speak of Augy as their brother with other people outside of the family. The children resented their father for this and never forgot it. As Augy got older, Phillip, Sr. blended him into the sanatorium as a staff worker, and no one there ever questioned it.

Phillip, Sr. slowly made his way back to his feet, a web of broken blood vessels emerging from just below the surface of the skin on his face. He felt inside his mouth to see if his teeth were still intact, spitting a mouthful of blood onto the floor.

"That make you feel better, son?" asked Phillip, Sr. with a snarky tone.

Phillip, Jr. laughed. "You got some hard nerves, old man, I'll give you that." Then motioned to Augy to put the false wall back in position over the steel door, which he did right away. He pointed to the doorway leading to the backside of the kitchen which his father slowly headed toward.

The group passed through the empty kitchen, out through the small cafeteria, and into the main connecting corridor. Phillip, Sr. looked to his son to indicate which way he should walk and then continued in the direction they chose.

All three brothers followed closely behind their father as they made their way in the direction of his interior offices, and, as they walked, something occurred to Dr. Killiecrankie. None of the other staff members were anywhere to be seen. In fact, patients who posed zero threat to others and would normally walk freely amongst the halls of this institution were nowhere in sight. For the first time since the early years of the sanatorium, it felt empty.

The sensation was eerie.

"What have you done with the other staff members? The patients?" asked Phillip Sr as he continued down the labyrinth of halls.

"That is no longer your concern, father. Keep walking," Phillip, Jr. responded in a cold, emotionless voice while using the barrel of his revolver to nudge the doctor along. He told his father to make the turn around the nearest corner and the group headed down the well-lit hallway that led to Observation Room B. Phillip, Jr. placed his left hand on his father's shoulder while simultaneously pressing the gun into his lower back.

"Don't move father..." he whispered into Phillip, Sr.'s ear as he slowly made his way around to face his father eye-to-eye. "You know this room well, don't you, father?" he asked.

Phillip Sr. glanced at the room and then back to his son and said, "What does any of this have to do-" Phillip, Jr. reached back and slammed the butt of the revolver onto his father's forehead.

"YOU DO NOT SPEAK! I AM THE ONE SPEAKING!"

Phillip Sr. fell to the ground quickly, at which point Augy leaned in and grabbed the doctor with his thick, muscular hands, built from years of manual labor, lifting him back to his feet with very little effort. He stood in front of his son, wobbly on his feet, trying his best to regain his balance, blood pouring from a massive open wound on his head.

Phillip, Jr., catching his breath and trying to compose himself but not having any success in doing so, began to speak in a frantic, anger-filled voice. "You remember a year ago in this very room Dad, little meeting you had with Lt. Col. Braxton...talking about the...little miracle of your research? Your little history maker? The apple of your eye. THAT LITTLE SON OF A..."

Morrison stepped in, placing his hand on his brother's shoulder, "Shhhhhh, shhh, shhh, it's okay. Breathe, brother, focus..."

Phillip, Jr. tucked the gun into his waistband at his back and regrouped. "I have watched you, year after year, patient after patient, constantly striving to find the next break in human evolution. You inspired me to chase that dream, as well. Both of us," he nodded to Morrison. "We followed in your footsteps. Were we slighted by your lack of affection and fatherly attention throughout the years? Absolutely, but like you've always told us with your research, 'the ends always justify the means.' It took a while for us to accept that fact, but once we did, we thought surely the work would give us that bond with you we deserved." A single stream of tears rolled down his cheek as years of built-up frustration finally made its way to the surface.

His hands gripped tighter and tighter. "You never gave us that recognition. Throughout all that we've done for you behind these walls, everything we've sacrificed...FOR YOU!" He paused, caught his breath, and continued. "So, when I see you spending hours, upon hours, upon hours, UPON HOURS! With that little kid, laughing and enjoying your time, rubbing it in our damn faces, maybe I just snapped!" Phillip, Jr. was laughing now, clearly going beyond any notion of self-control.

"Is that what this is all about?! Patient H7?" Dr. Killiecrankie was highly disappointed. "In all the years you have served under me in this very institution, I have experienced a number of emotions regarding you and your brothers. Frustration. Anger. Definitely regret. Truth be told, I never wanted to have children, not a single one of you. Your mother wanted a family, and I just wanted my work to blend in, so, a family we had. And it worked. But I thought to myself, 'Maybe, just maybe, these little whiny shits will grow up and become something useful' and boy, oh boy, was I wrong there! I mean look at the three of you...You know what I feel when I look at you? Embarrassment. Flat-out embarrassment. Look at you. What? 'Daddy didn't hold you enough when you were a kid?' You three are PATHETIC! JEALOUS OF A SEVEN-YEAR-OLD PATIENT!"

Morrison took the strap and whipped him three times across the back with as much strength and aggression as he could. "But he's not *just* a patient, is he?! He's your son!"

Phillip Sr. was in a lot of pain at this point, but he tried his best to maintain his balance so he could face his children with whatever shred of dignity he had left. He had pieced together a while back that his sons may have been harboring feelings of jealousy toward his relationship with Patient H7. Small jabs and cutting comments here and there about the time spent with the patient and the unwillingness to push for harder experimentation when other patients around the same age had historically experienced much tougher treatment sessions than Patient H7. For those other patients, it was always the same logic given; "the ends always justify the means." For Patient H7, Dr. Killiecrankie never seemed to want to push that limit, of which the brothers most definitely took notice and resented.

Being the work-driven, emotionally distant man that he was, he never picked up on the emotional toll that his character was taking on his sons, and because of that obliviousness to their emotional anguish, he never once considered that maybe they knew about his infidelity which bore a son. That was what really brought out the resentment.

"How did you find out?" he asked of his sons, never denying the accusation. Phillip, Jr. slowly walked backward and motioned for his father to follow, which he did. He stopped at a set of office doors and recounted the day Lt. Col. Braxton arrived, and, when he left, how he overheard his conversation with Nurse Rucker in the hallway.

A look fell over Phillip Sr.'s face as if to say, "Of course." All was clear to him now, and there was no denying any of the truth that had been revealed. He instead tried to justify his actions, which had a very negative outcome.

"You're absolutely right, son. Patient H7 is biologically my son... and Nurse Rucker is biologically his mother. Those are undeniable facts. But you're trying to make this out to be some nefarious plot that I concocted to somehow replace you and your brothers with a different, younger version. There are factors here that you're *clearly* not aware of. Patient H7 is a test subject. That's all he has been to me..."

"And what about Nurse Rucker? Your cute little mistress on the side while our dear, sick mother rots away at home?

What about her?! Do you feel anything for her? Or are you gonna try and pretend she's nothing more than a test subject, too?" Phillip, Jr. quickly jabbed back.

Phillip Sr. stood still, not responding right away. Before he could think of what to say, Phillip, Jr. said, "You said it yourself, old man, you never wanted a single one of us. We were just a cover to take away attention from your work. So just say it… you never cared about us or Mom. Say it!"

Dr. Phillip Killiecrankie, Sr. stood in that hallway in front of his three sons and felt the sensation of what most people felt moments before they knew they were going to die. Images of his life flashed before his eyes, and he could feel that, in a matter of minutes, it would be over. The time for talking had ticked away. The act of bargaining was off the table. All that was left was truth. He had nothing else to give his sons.

"In all of my life, I have never seen grown men appear so small and insignificant. You stand here and ask me to tell you the truth. Well, here are the last ounces of truth you will ever get from me. Your mother is a good woman, and she loved me despite all of my character flaws, but your mother was also a fool for marrying me…"

The brothers became agitated.

Phillip Sr. continued, "I never loved her. I never loved any of you. What, actually, is love? A chemical reaction inside the brain? It never existed in me for any of you. Especially your mother. She could not give me in a thousand lifetimes what I got from Nurse Rucker. Your mom wanted a family…she can have you. You'll have to watch her slowly die in her bed at home. I wanted to reshape the world, and Nurse Rucker gave me that when she gave birth to Patient H7, and, because of him, my research will live on well after I'm gone. And to think, he has shown more potential in his short seven years than any one of you three will ever have in your small, pathetic, lives. I truly hope that's what you wanted to hear!" The old man was laughing at this point.

Phillip, Jr.'s face became blood red. His anger was palpable, it could almost be heard echoing off the walls of the hallway. He desperately wanted to kill his father right then and there, but that wasn't part of the plan. Instead, he grabbed his father by the jacket pulling him close, and said, "What happens in the next few seconds will determine how brutal your death is. Where, are your patient files for the military project and which former patient was Nurse Rucker going to see? Tell me right now..."

Hearing the questions, Phillip Sr. then realized that his sons didn't have all the answers ahead of time, and all of his work would be safe until one day, someone other than his children would discover the files and set out to have his research continued and his sons held accountable for their crimes. He laughed directly in the face of his son and said, "You really don't know anything, do you? Just as I've always thought about you...nothing!"

"TELL ME!" Phillip, Jr. screamed at the top of his lungs.

Undaunted, Phillip Sr. responded, "Go to hell, son. I'll save you a seat."

That was the straw that broke the camel's back.

The line had been crossed.

His time had come.

Phillip, Jr. pulled his father further down the hall to a large, wooden door with a series of latches marked "A6." "Augy! The door!"

The larger brother stomped forward, opening all the latches, and then held the doorknob, waiting for the signal. Phillip, Jr. leaned in close to his father, whispering in his ear, "I'd love nothing more than to watch *you* die slowly, but I guess we're all feeling a little bit of disappointment today. But that's okay, father. I'll feel a lot better once you're gone, and I can resume treatments on your little bundle of joy, Patient H7. And don't worry about pretty Miss Rucker, your little mistress. Morrison has some very interesting plans for her."

Phillip Sr. felt tightness in his heart and rage in his blood.

"Oh, I almost forgot...your precious work and your research will never live on. You, wanna know why? Because we already have a plan to make sure that your name never survives history. You will only ever be known as the man who was killed by his own patients!"

Augy flung open the door while Phillip, Jr. pushed their father into the patient room.

Inside, there were four patient beds anchored to the floors with disheveled bed linens and unkempt mattresses. In the middle of the room were two activity tables, six feet apart, also anchored to the floor, and just beyond them stood four patients who quickly turned to see the doctor standing there.

They were the most violent of patients to have ever been admitted, and their aggressive tendencies had only increased throughout the past decade of their stay due to the experimentations administered. Only, Phillip Sr. hadn't been administering those particular sessions; his sons had. Prior to their separation from the facility, they had increased their levels of experimentation on the violent patients to satisfy their sick, internal desires, and because of that, the patients had reached maximum levels of rage.

The four patients had cuts and bruises and torn gowns from where they had been attacking each other for the past hour. The brothers had removed the straight jackets from each patient and left them free of restraints in the room so that their aggression would build.

Now, it was time to use them as a weapon.

The door closed behind Killiecrankie. He frantically tried his best to open it, but Augy was quickly locking each latch in succession. The brothers stood outside the door, listening to their father hopelessly pleading with the patients who were too far gone to comprehend anything he was saying to them. The assault was brutal, and his screams were piercing. It was only a matter of minutes before the founder of the Western Kentucky Rehabilitation and Sanatorium had been beaten to death in his own facility.

The brothers stood quietly in the hallway for a few minutes after the attack ended, finally fulfilling the plan they had devised the year prior. A sense of satisfaction floated in the space between the three men and at once, they all stood straight and decided to get to the next phase of their plan.

"There's no time to waste, brothers. Augy, move all the patients down to the new expansion and make sure they are all secure. Morris, you gather all the staff together from outside and bring them to the cafeteria. We'll see who wants to be a part of the new administration here at the Asylum. Once we have everyone in place, I'll initiate lock-down, and we'll scour this place with a fine-toothed comb and find those files." instructed Phillip, Jr.

"Nurse Rucker?" asked Morrison.

"We have time on our hands now. We can play later."

"What should we do with the staffers who resist?"

"Sedate half of them and make them into new patients. I have some new 'treatments' I've been wanting to try out. The other half... get Augy to help you bring them here, and we'll see how they fair locked in a room with our fathers' *murderers*," he pretended to wipe away a tear. "I'm in mourning, you know," he said as he started laughing, with Morrison just shaking his head.

Then the smile faded, and his tone shifted dramatically.

"Little brothers, when father began his treatments on Patient H7, he thought he created someone that would change the world. When we're finished with H7 and all these other patients, we'll show the world what he really created..."

"...a reckoning."

Chapter Five
"Half Day"

City of Henderson
July 15, 1986 | 3:58 P.M.

The sheriff's patrol car raced down Highway 60 as fast as the lawman could push the motor, sirens blaring a screeching cry of authority out into the warm, country air with the lights engaged on the roof of the car casting out a visual warning to drivers ahead to *"Steer clear, the police are on the hunt!"*

The field trip to the remains of the Western Kentucky Rehabilitation and Sanatorium facility had been more than fruitful; it had been incredibly eye-opening. So much information had seeped into the foundation of this case from various locations, physically and historically, that lines for motive and causality had been not only blurred but they had also blown to oblivion by the winds of irrational thought. Nothing about this case seemed logical, yet everything was somehow starting to connect. However, the shades of gray that danced along the fringes of truth on the case were starting to wane on Whittaker, and he wanted to clear the waters of this case, immediately.

All three men, Sheriff Dobson, Deputy Martin, and SA Whittaker sat quietly in the speeding car, processing everything they had experienced to that point. On the surface, one would guess that they were all focused on the same subject, but when Dobson peeked in his rear-view mirror at Whittaker, it was obvious that was not the case.

"How did you do it, Whittaker?" he asked bluntly.

"How did I do what?" Whittaker responded, never turning his head as he stared at the houses whipping by on the side of the highway.

"The box in the wall...the Killiecrankie files...all of it! How did you know they were there? How the hell could you have possibly known about the hidden section of the asylum?"

"I was just thinking the same thing," Martin chimed in.

"How the hell did you two know about the hidden part of the asylum?" Whittaker said. "I was more surprised by the lack of response from you two than when I actually found it. You two had definitely been in that space before, and you weren't going to say a thing about it till I found it. Which tells me you guys are hiding something..."

"You walk into a space you claim to have never been in before..."

"Claim?" questioned Whittaker.

"Within minutes, you walk through a series of rooms and hallways directly to a doorway that leads to a section of the old building that isn't quite common knowledge, and then, to top off that magic trick, you bust out your finale by conveniently finding a box of very incriminating evidence that, allegedly, no one knew about for over twenty years..."

"Allegedly!" Whittaker was now leaning forward in his seat,

glaring back at Dobson.

"All you need now is a top hat and a pretty assistant so you can go 'TA-DA!!' and wait for your applause. You seem very suspicious to me, Whittaker!"

"In a case that's as murky as this one, when you have no suspect and no clear motive, everything becomes suspicious. I could say the same thing about you, Dobson, and trust me, after we deal with the Killiecrankies, we're going to sort this out. But for now, let's focus on the only lead we have."

Sheriff Dobson didn't respond but continued driving.

They were now entering the city limits and heading right into the heart of town. Henderson was a small town, but it had seen steady growth over the years due to the increase of industrial prospects in the spacious, accommodating county. Plenty of land, plenty of tax breaks, and an eager working class looking to financially solidify their retirement plans were as textbook as an equation to successfully building a small-town economy.

At the center of all this growth were the good, down-to-earth citizens who helped bring it all together to make a community. The Killiecrankie Brothers had used this community and its small-town charm to hide whatever their motives were in plain sight. It was time for someone to pull back the curtain on the brothers and see what their intentions had been all along.

Upon entering the city, the patrol car blared through a busy four-lane road, past the fast-food restaurants, and into a residential area. The north end of the neighborhood met with an area where there were various medical offices, including the hospital, but halfway down were a series of older, much larger homes that had been built in the earlier part of the century. Beautiful two and three-story homes overlooking the river in a neat little row down a beautiful thoroughfare adorned with large oak trees.

Parked in front of one of these houses was another patrol car. Deputy Harkins. As Sheriff Dobson slowed to a stop behind the car, Harkins came sprinting from the open front door of the house. All three men saw this and quickly exited the vehicle, drawing their weapons.

"ONE SUSPECT DOWN, ANOTHER IN THE HOUSE!" Harkins screamed.

Whittaker, Dobson, and Martin ran into the yard, mobilizing with Harkins and the four men made their way back to the house, taking cover and looking for clear sight lines.

"What the hell is going on, Harkins?" Dobson asked.

"Dr. Killiecrankie is dead! Engaged one suspect and got jumped from behind by the other suspect..."

"Which doctor?" Whittaker asked in the commotion.

"Morrison..." he replied, almost out of breath. He had a small trickle of blood running down through his hairline by his right ear from a half-inch gash.

Whittaker was taken aback by the news. All the evidence they had pieced together at this point had become nothing more than a swaying pendulum of suspects and motives, but who was truly at the center of the mystery swinging the pendulum?

It was at this point, the sound of rapid footsteps reverberated from the front doorway as a man wearing a dirty, wrinkled patient gown with blood streaks across his chest, darted down the front steps, holding a large knife above his head and running directly at Deputy Martin.

The deputy paused, only for a split second, then aimed his firearm at the man, firing a single shot that hit its mark, center mast, taking the suspect down immediately.

Sheriff Dobson quickly got on his radio, calling for additional police presence and medical personnel.

Harkins verified that the man Deputy Martin shot was the second suspect.

Within seconds, Harkins and Whittaker had moved back up the steps to the front door, taking the initiative to sweep the house for other suspects. Due to the size of the house, it took a few minutes, but once they were satisfied no one else was inside, they gave the "all clear" to the rest of the officers and began processing the scene.

Within fifteen minutes of the initial encounter, the entire block was covered with police, fire, and medical personnel. Nearby families were questioned of suspicious characters and activities which turned up no leads. Odd, considering it was during daytime hours, which, in this part of the country, summertime sunshine can fill the sky until close to 9 pm on a clear day. Neighbors were told to shelter in place until the initial investigation was completed, and city police began searching the neighborhood for any leads or possible evidence.

Out on the front lawn of Morrison Killiecrankie's home,

which also acted as his private practice, the body of the assailant that Deputy Martin shot was processed, covered, and removed by the coroner.

Inside the home, a violent scene was laid out like an open book for the Sheriff's Office, city police, and Medical Examiner. Forced entry at the side door from the driveway led to a brief scuffle in the hallway that spilled into the front living room.

Furniture had been knocked over, blood spatter could be seen on the walls and carpet, and skin tissue was found embedded into the edge of the carpet going back into the hallway. A dragging trail of blood from the hardwood in the hallway led through the kitchen into a sunroom that had been converted into an exam room, more than likely Morrison's private practice, and through another doorway that led downstairs to the basement.

It was a fully-finished basement, nearly the same square footage as the first floor, but with one distinctive feature that stood out from most ordinary basements.

One industrial-strength steel door leading to an extra room.

The door had been unlocked and left open when Harkins first discovered it and inside, strapped down to a waist-high, wooden workbench, Morrison Killiecrankie lay on his belly, dead. The entire surface area of skin on his back had been completely beaten away. On the ground next to the workbench, another man in a dingy, wrinkled-up patient gown, lay deceased in a mixed pool of his and Morrison's blood with two rounds plug in his chest. A blood-soaked leather strap was nearby with one end tied tightly around the dead suspect's wrist, apparently done so in an effort to not lose grip when using the strap against Morrison.

According to an initial viewing of the body, the ME determined that Morrison died from blood loss and shock from the trauma inflicted to his back. The majority of the injuries were inflicted well after he had passed. Another gruesome message was sent out into the world by an unknown harbinger.

While the ME's finished processing the bloody scene in the basement, upstairs, Deputy Harkins gave a recount to the other three of what happened leading up to his encounter at the residence.

"I did what you said, Whittaker. I drove to both brothers' medical practices to ask them to come in and answer some questions. I came here first, and no one answered. I noticed a car in the driveway, so I went around back because that's where he has his office and the door was locked, curtains closed, with no answer. So, I left and drove to Phillip's office, and the same thing, no answer. A handwritten note taped to the inside of the door that said, "Half Day. Sorry for the inconvenience." I recognized his car in the spot out front, so I thought it was odd that he didn't answer."

"You didn't think to radio to us and let us know?" asked Dobson.

"I was about to when something caught my attention."

"What was that?'" asked Whittaker.

"I noticed a beat-up, maintenance truck with 'Tranquil Meadows Health' painted on the side pulling out from behind Killiecrankie's medical office and heading south. With neither one of them answering at their private offices, the truck reminded me of the health facility, so I figured maybe one or both of the brothers may be doing official office hours at the old folks home, so I followed the truck. The paint had faded pretty badly, but I could still make out the logo and some of the letters. One thing that really stuck out was the license plate...it was so dirty I couldn't make out the full tag. When it got to the building, the truck went around back and pulled into a service garage and the door was quickly shut."

"Did you go inside and ask for the doctors?" asked Dobson.

"Affirmative, sir. I was greeted by the receptionist at the front desk. She told me that neither one of the doctors was there and hadn't been there all day... which I just felt was odd. Something about it didn't sit right with me, so I pressed her on it." said Harkins.

"And? What did she say?" Whittaker asked, impatiently.

"She acted peculiar. Like she wasn't sure what to say. Then she just blurted out that she forgot that Dr. Morrison *had* been there earlier but then said he was going home and just left ten minutes prior. The more I looked at her, the more I didn't recognize her. She just seemed out of place, so I asked her if she was new. She kind of fumbled over her words and then finally said she was just volunteering at the facility. I didn't really have any reason to not believe her. She just seemed like an awkward person. With a smile that seemed too forced. Just awkward. I gave her the number for the sheriff's office and told her to have either of the doctors call us if they showed up."

"Was that it?" Whittaker asked in a deflated tone.

Harkins stood there quietly as if he were trying to make sense of something in his head. The quizzical look on his face caught everyone's attention.

"Just say it Harkins, use your damn words, kid!" said Martin.

"Sir... I might be imagining it, but I got the feeling that there wasn't anyone in Tranquil Meadows. The doors leading into the interior hallways were closed, which they never are usually, and I couldn't hear anyone or anything. Like everyone had been moved out of the main building."

Dobson shifted uncomfortably at this detail and slowly rubbed both of his forearms as if a cool breeze had just blown over him. That detail wasn't lost on Whittaker, but he let Harkins continue his report.

"It felt closed but the parking lot was full and that volunteer was up front. I don't know, I'm probably making something out of nothing. Anyway, the doctors weren't there, so I decided to try Morrison's house again since the girl said he had just left. I got two blocks away and dispatch radioed for me saying that my brother had stopped by the office to talk to me."

"I don't see how that's relevant, Harkins," noted Dobson.

"I don't have a brother, sir," replied Harkins.

The hair on the necks of the other three men stood at attention.

"I went to the office not knowing what to expect, and when I got there, a tall, lanky man wearing one of those stupid patient gowns was standing outside the office, just smiling. Nothing else. He never spoke one word. He just stood there smiling at me."

"Please tell me you arrested him, forcefully," said Martin.

"We're holding him on a couple of made-up misdemeanor charges. I didn't feel safe letting him go, especially knowing what happened next."

The three men waited for him to continue.

"We get two separate calls on 911 claiming to be children of the Killiecrankie brothers, and they think their fathers are missing, and they suspect foul play."

"I thought neither of them married or had children?" Dobson asked.

"That's because they didn't, sir," said Harkins.

"Someone is trying to distract us," commented Whittaker.

"Well, I knew something wasn't adding up, and that's when I radioed you, sir. I headed over to Morrison's house for the second time but when I got there this time, the front door was wide open. I hurried up to the door with my weapon drawn, and from the steps, all I saw was wreckage and blood. I don't know what came over me. I just acted, you know? I followed the trail of blood down to the basement, and that's when I discovered the doctor. The man had already beaten him to death. He was still beating him with that damn strap. Over and over and over again. Why was he doing that? He was so distracted by what he was doing, that he didn't even know I was there till I identified myself. That's when he turned and came at me. I didn't have a moment to think…I just... shot...."

Harkins paused, staring off into nothingness, fixated on the memory burned in his mind. He snapped from his trance and the emotions flooded to the surface. "I didn't wait for backup. I should've waited. I'm sorry, sir. I should've waited..."

His recollection of the encounter was starting to become all too real in his memory. At the time, adrenaline helped make the situation more navigable, but here, retelling it from his thoughts, was a different story now that the adrenaline had worn off.

"No, no, Harkins, you are alright. You did alright, son," said Sheriff Dobson, resting his hand on his deputy's shoulder to help him realize that these are the tough decisions you have to face as a lawman.

Even Martin, as indifferent as he can come across at times, stepped forward and patted his young partner on the back to show his support.

Harkins took a deep breath and said, "After I shot the perp, the second guy came out of nowhere with a knife and got me on the head. We scuffled back and forth, and when I freed myself, I made a run for the door. I guess I thought that if there was one extra guy I didn't know about, then there could be more. That's when you guys showed up, and you know the rest. Excuse me for a second." Harkins excused himself to step outside and let a first responder look at his wound.

The others followed.

Outside, the sun was slowly making its journey to the horizon, and, in a few hours, dusk would take over for a period before nightfall reclaimed its hold on the sky. The air was still hot, but it wasn't as thick as earlier. A slight breeze rolled through the tree branches above and the men took a moment to collectively catch their breaths.

After the EMS worker gave the "thumbs up" to Harkins, he rejoined them in a section of the front yard away from the other officers and first responders so the group could speak candidly without anyone eavesdropping.

The day felt like it would never end, and so much had happened in such a short time that the heaviness of it all was starting to wear on the men. Whittaker had come to this town with the intention of maybe, hopefully, getting some information that may help his case back in Fredericksburg. Never did he imagine that this trip would put him right in the thick of mysterious circumstances that had plagued this small town for decades.

He needed answers, and he needed them right now.

"Sheriff, I think you can appreciate the gravity of what is happening all around us right now. There are forces working together that have us on the front step of something huge; I truly believe that."

Dobson stood stoically, not speaking.

Whittaker continued, "I want to share something with you that I've never told anyone else. It's something that I've been afraid to talk about before but...this case...being here and learning everything we've learned...I feel like I've been brought here for a reason. By some unknown force. It's hard for me to explain, but, I want to try. I *want* to trust you all with this, but, you've gotta give me something in return, Sheriff. You're holding back something, I can feel that. What is it?"

Sheriff Dobson folded his arms, not sure how to respond.

Deputy Martin kept shooting glances at him as if he were fully anticipating the floodgates to open and Harkins was completely in the dark, waiting patiently with everyone else.

Over in the driveway, the coroner was spotted moving the body of Morrison Killiecrankie, clearly finished with processing the scene from the steel-doored room in the basement. Soon, the second body belonging to the assailant would be brought out.

Whittaker was still waiting for a response that didn't come.

"Fine...whatever, you don't want to talk about it. Let's just talk about what happened here. Any thoughts on who planned all this out?" Whittaker asked, shifting the conversation.

"My money is on the brother, Phillip, Jr. He's got access to patients, he's medically trained, and he's probably cutting off loose ends considering the note we found with the files," Martin offered as his motive and theory.

Harkins looked confused, "What files?"

Whittaker quickly gave him a recap of the events out at the

asylum that led to the discovery of the old files in the wall.

"Well, yeah, I like Martin's theory, then. Makes sense to me," Harkins added.

"Well, by that assertion, that means you like Phillip, Jr. for the murder of Lt. Col. Braxton, too. Remember, there are details with the murders and missing persons cases that directly link to my murder investigation and many disappearances heading toward the East Coast. If we're going to make that link, then we have to have a clear-cut motive. Morrison Killiecrankie, sure, I can kind of see it, but Braxton? What would be his motive for killing Braxton in such a horrific way? And remember what was scrawled on the wall with Braxton's blood? *"Your sins will soon be on display...."* What would Phillip, Jr. consider Braxton's sins to be? I think the doctor is involved in this somehow, and it's probably not from a place of innocence, but we need more than just speculation at this point."

"You left out the part where you somehow mysteriously found a hidden space behind a false wall that apparently nobody knew about for the past two decades," Dobson interjected.

Whittaker didn't balk at the jab.

"And you're still leaving out pieces to a puzzle that no one knows what the picture is," Whittaker said with a very determined voice.

Sheriff Dobson, who had been rather aloof in his conversations with Whittaker all day, finally caved and allowed a bit of water through the dam.

"What if the military *is* the connection, Whittaker?" he offered.

Whittaker surprised to see Dobson finally joining the party, quickly responded. "I would think that if the military were involved in this situation then the FBI would know about it, and there would be no need to send me in to investigate. They would have to be in on it, which would beg the question, 'Why send one of their best agents to solve a murder investigation of someone that would be implicated in a much larger set of nefarious circumstances that they are already aware of?' It would be foolish to put me on the case and naive of them to think I wouldn't figure it out."

"You're operating under the assumption that the FBI *would* know about military involvement." Dobson chimed in, teasing a thread that he knows Whittaker is desperate to pull.

Whittaker gave a crooked grin.

Dobson was finally loosening up.

"I knew you knew something....tell me. Tell me."

Over on the driveway, the Medical Examiner had just exited the house and yelled out for Sheriff Dobson. All four men made their way to the ME who updated them that the initial processing of the crime scene was complete and that they were free to investigate the scene as they needed.

As he spoke, the body of the assailant from the basement that Harkins had shot was carefully wheeled out by the coroner. The workers stopped the gurney next to the men to sign off on paperwork, and Harkins looked blankly at the dead body. It was his first "on-duty" shooting, and he wasn't sure how to feel about it. He had done his job, but he had also taken a life. The walk he was taking on that double-edged sword was certainly no walk in the park.

Deputy Martin took one step forward toward the body. It was fully covered so as not to upset the proverbial "looky-loos" of the neighborhood, but the left arm had shifted from under the covering, revealing a dirt and blood-stained patient's gown. Martin clutched the gown between his index finger and his thumb, feeling the material, and recalling a memory. He turned back to the group and under his breath he whispered to himself, "This can't be happening again."

Whittaker caught it and was just about to call him out on it when the ME turned to them and said, "Oh, just wanted to give you the heads up, be careful when you go into the room where the crime scene took place. The suspect apparently used the victim's blood to write a message on the wall above the door. There's blood everywhere."

"What was the written message?" asked Sheriff Dobson.

A swirling vortex whipped up inside Whittaker's mind, pulling him close as the dark void reappeared, and, out of the darkness, the voice spoke the chilling words....

"FINAL TREATMENT."

Whittaker spoke the words just as the medical examiner did, who was surprised.

"That's right. 'Final Treatment.' I guess you already saw the crime scene? I'd say 'Final Treatment' is right considering everyone is dead," he said, cackling to himself as he helped the coroner take away the body.

Martin and Harkins looked at Whittaker out of curiosity, and Dobson looked at him like a veteran officer interrogating a prime suspect.

"THAT! That right there! You have been doing that all day, now. Now what is going on with you because if you're not a suspect, you're damn sure a person of interest at this point, and I want an explanation!" Dobson roared out at the Special Agent.

Whittaker calmly and coolly responded, "Oh no, Sheriff… I'll show you mine if you show me yours."

Dobson fumed and would've blown his top, but Deputy Martin leaned in and whispered, "Sheriff... you gotta tell him. He has to know before we go any further..."

Whittaker was pleasantly surprised to see Martin take the initiative. Their day had started in a rather "standoffish-pissing match" kind of way, but it was clear that Martin had the same objective as Whittaker: solving the case.

Dobson took a beat, then said, "We can't talk here."

The veteran sheriff motioned for them to follow him back to his patrol car, making sure no one else was in earshot. Once he was satisfied that they had a safe space, he stared point-blank at Whittaker and began to unload the burden he had been carrying for years.

"Before I say anything, I want your word that this conversation goes no further than this circle, you understand? It's important you give me your word."

Whittaker and Harkins both agreed as Deputy Martin stood with a pained expression on his face. He clearly knew what the sheriff was about to relay to the other two men, and he was not thrilled about reliving the details.

"Okay then. Everything you know about the asylum you have gotten from police reports and old newspaper clippings. But what you don't know about are the details that the military covered up..."

Whittaker sat back on the trunk of the car and let the sheriff continue.

"In January of 1963, I hadn't been a deputy but maybe a year, year and a half. It had been nice because there wasn't a ton of crime in this area at the time, especially out in the county. Domestic arguments call from time to time, but nothing major. About the only crazy crime I'd witnessed was Delbert Jenkins getting drunk and shooting his tractor with a shotgun when it broke down in his wheat field!"

Dobson snickered at the memory, as did the others.

It was a nice moment that broke up the seriousness of the day that each man needed and appreciated, but his tone quickly returned to the business at hand.

He continued, "I'm in the office one day, and we get a call from a guy who lives down the road from the asylum. He says there's a delivery truck driver at this door asking if he knows when the facility opens...says he's been trying to drop off his delivery of medical supplies for three days, and no one has been at the building. They ask if someone from the sheriff's office could run out to the asylum and check it out. I had nothing going on at the moment, so I volunteered to make the run. The delivery driver meets me at the end of the lane and follows me out to the building. After we park at the main entrance, he tells me that the asylum is a regular run for him, comes about every four or five months or so to drop off a large shipment of medical supplies, and this was the first time in his five years that he wasn't able to make the drop-off. Said no one called his company to put a stop to the delivery either. So, the both of us spend the next twenty minutes going from door-to-door, window-to-window, looking for someone or a way to get in. That's when I find an unlocked exterior door on the west end of the building that leads into a storage room attached to a small corridor of extra administrative offices. I tell you, when I think back to the moment I stepped inside the main hallway of the asylum, it makes my blood run cold."

Dobson took a moment, visibly shivering at the very thought. The others gave him time to compose himself.

"I felt like I was walking alone through a graveyard. I had never heard a building so quiet before in my life. It was like the life had been completely sucked out of it. I had instructed the delivery driver to stay outside because I wasn't sure what to expect inside. I wasn't expecting anything dangerous...I guess I figured I would eventually run into someone, and it would be a huge misunderstanding or lack of communication, so I just kept walking through the halls. Office after office, room after room, nothing...until I made my way down the corridor that trailed off from Dr. Killiecrankie's office to the Observation Rooms we saw earlier today."

Whittaker nodded and Dobson kept talking. "I could hear... something. I didn't know what it was. It didn't sound natural, but it got louder and louder as I kept on down the hallway. I came to a solid door with several latches on the outside labeled "'A6,'" and I could hear the noise very loudly from inside. It sounded like growling but not like a dog or a bear. I wasn't sure what to do, and, against my better judgment, I decided to open the door. I thought to myself, if it's a wild animal I will just put it down."

He paused and then said, "I opened the door, and inside, on the ground, a very large man in a dingy, bloody patient's gown was hovered over top of a dead body, eating away the skin off the corpse's face. I was in shock, but when I drew my firearm, the patient heard me, turned his attention toward me, and started to run straight at me! I emptied the pistol and dropped him instantly. After I was able to pull myself back together, that's when I was able to really see the horrible scene in that room. Counting the patients I had just shot, there were eight total bodies in that room. Four of them were patients, three of them were staff members, and the last one was Dr. Phillip Killiecrankie, Sr."

Special Agent Whittaker was stunned. What an insane revelation and none of it was present in any report filed by the Henderson County Sheriff's Office. He had so many questions and wasn't quite sure how to take the story that was just laid out before him, but he could tell that Dobson wasn't finished, so he bit his tongue and waited.

"I found out after the fact that the four patients were violent-natured patients and everyone else had been locked inside with them and left to die. They beat the doctor and the staff members to death and then fed off of them for months. One of the staffers was the janitor, Jake Miller. I knew him...went to school with him...nice guy. Couldn't identify him by his body which was completely destroyed, but I saw the uniform and his name tag. Terrible. The gunshots must have scared the delivery driver because, by the time I had made it back outside, he had split. I immediately radioed it in to my superiors, and, within the half hour, every available deputy was there investigating the property. We had state and local officials there, going over the property, trying to locate staff members...it was an absolute circus. What we couldn't figure out was what happened to the other patients. What happened to everyone else? The investigation went well into the night when around midnight, a black Lincoln Continental pulled up to the property and out steps two men, one of which who immediately took over the scene. Clearly military, I had no idea why he would be there, and I sure as hell had no clue how he got there so quickly! That's when I realized that there was way more going on here outside of a stack of homicides. I was instructed to keep my distance from the scene by my superiors, but since I was the one who made the discovery, I got pulled into an office inside the asylum and grilled for hours by two representatives of the United States Military. I'll give you one guess who was in charge," he said to Whittaker.

SA Whittaker was staring at the ground, shaking his head when he slowly raised his head and said, "Colonel Will Braxton, am I right?"

"*Lieutenant* Colonel Braxton back then. Needless to say, the entire situation was covered up, and I was instructed to keep my mouth shut. Cover stories were filtered out to news outlets, and by the time it hit the county, the official story was that the asylum had been closed by the state when it was discovered that Dr. Killiecrankie was killed by a patient who had accidentally been left loose from restraints. They conveniently left out the dead staff members, the discovery of the gruesome scene, and the officer-involved shooting of an asylum patient. All the gruesome, gory details were redacted for the cover story to not upset the general public. In the cover story, all other patients had been moved out of state to other facilities when, in reality, they had no damn clue where those patients were. Staff members whose bodies were discovered were covered up. We were instructed to file missing persons cases on each one, perform due diligence on them for a few years, and then shift them to cold case files. For any patient that extended family members came calling for, they were told that they had been moved or unfortunately passed under the facility's care. They even made up fake death certificates! He had me in an asylum office for hours just to make sure I knew to go along with their cover-up if I didn't want anything to happen to me. Whittaker, they had files on every single one of us in the Sheriff's Office back then. All of us. We knew back then what would happen if any of us fessed up to what was going on. And when I asked Braxton why the United States Military would go through all this trouble...you know what his answer was?"

"When dealing with matters of 'National Security,' the ends always justify the means."

"That's government-speak for 'We're covering our asses,' said Dobson.

The group fell silent, taking in the massive amount of history that Sheriff Dobson had just laid out.

After a few moments, he spoke again, "When you called our offices and told me whose murder you were investigating and the details surrounding it, I got scared. Really scared. Because if someone out there knew he was involved, then they probably know I aided in covering it up, and it would be a matter of time before they come for me too. Add onto that the rash of new missing persons followed up by missing persons turning up dead. I'm just sorry I waited so long to tell you. Then again...we've only just met today," Dobson said with a weak smile.

"It has been a very long day," Whittaker said, returning a smile.

He was beside himself hearing the history from Sheriff Dobson, and he trusted every word of it. This certainly changed things regarding the Special Agent's case.

They all stood next to the patrol car, contemplating their next move, when Whittaker remembered something that was said. "Deputy Martin... what did you mean when you said, 'This can't be happening again.'?"

"When did I say that?" asked Martin.

Whittaker reminded him that he said it when the coroner wheeled out the dead suspect.

"You felt the patient gown, got lost in thought, then muttered that statement as you walked off. I heard you."

Martin looked to Dobson for quick guidance when Whittaker started in again, "You weren't even on the force in '63... Hell, I don't even think you were out of junior high when all of that stuff went down, so you saying that wouldn't make sense. What am I missing here, gentlemen?"

Dobson looked at Martin as if to say, *Don't worry, I'll take this one*, then moved closer to Whittaker.

Harkins leaned in closer to hear and Martin just stood off to the side, silent.

Sheriff Dobson took a quick look around and then said, "You know how I said the military covered everything up in 1963?"

Whittaker nodded.

"They had to come back in 1975 and do it again."

A chill shot up Whittaker's spine as he asked, "What happened in 1975?"

"All those missing patients from the asylum. They weren't missing...they were hidden. In 1975, all of those patients reappeared, and we were not prepared for how they would return."

Chapter Six
"Tormerdol"

After the grizzly discovery of what had become of Dr. Phillip Killiecrankie, Sr., followed by the subsequent cover-up by the US Military in early 1963, the family name "Killiecrankie" dredged up two different types of emotions throughout the community in Henderson County.

Some felt empathy for the brothers, who had been doing a really good job of playing the "pillar-of-the-community, grief-stricken sons" of the deceased doctor. Along with that, there were those in the county who used the chilling local news story as a means to perpetuate horror stories of the darkest creativity while also conjuring up bald-faced lies about the doctor and the facility. Then there were the "down home" folk who just couldn't believe something so mortifying would happen right there in their community that they flat-out refused to talk about it. They hoped that time would slowly erase the stories *and* the building from history.

The cover stories had been set in place to keep people from investigating and to also temper the potential of blowback onto the Defense Department, which had originally sanctioned the contract between the US Military and Dr.

Killiecrankie. If word got out of the arrangement and what research had really taken place behind those doors of the sanatorium, the public outcry would have been deafening. It was definitely in the interest of the military to make damn sure no one knew the truth of what happened out there. Part of that was pulling some strings on the move for the State of Kentucky to officially take control of the property and have it on record as condemned.

The first hiccup in the military's plan to distance themselves from the failure of the asylum occurred in the middle part of 1963, only a handful of months after the discovery of Phillip, Sr. While sitting in his office in Washington, D.C., Lt. Col. Braxton looked over his messages that had come in that morning before his arrival.

At the bottom of the stack, a letter sent via the Postal Service with a Spottsville, KY postmark took him by surprise. Dr. Killiecrankie was dead, the agreement with the military disavowed, and all relevant files associated with the program stamped, filed, and locked away in an archive in the deepest recesses of the Pentagon. There would be no real reason for correspondence at this juncture.

He looked at the unmarked envelope addressed to him, paused, and then carefully opened the letter. Inside, a small, 3x3 cut piece of paper had typed printing, perfectly centered, that read:

"McArthur's Deli - July 11th - 10 am - New Deal?"

It only took a brief second for the Lt. Col. to piece together who had sent the letter. He glanced at the clock on the wall that read 9:17 am. It was July 11th. He took a small breath, then stood up from his desk, put his jacket on, and made out for the deli.

After arriving early, Braxton sat in a corner booth facing the front of the deli, which was completely open with large, floor-to-ceiling windows that swung out illuminating the entire establishment with natural light. Outside, his assistant stood guard by the door, and, on the inside, the deli was empty, compliments of the power of the United States Military. He passed the time by stirring his cup of coffee with a spoon when, right at five till, in walked Phillip, Jr. and Morrison Killiecrankie.

The brothers spotted Braxton and casually strolled over, sliding into the booth on the opposite side. They gave courtesy greetings to the Lt. Col. and then sat in silence.

Braxton made the first gesture of conversation. "Gentlemen, you wanted this meeting...so, speak."

"Yes, well, we never got the opportunity to thank you in person for everything you've done for our family and the work at the sanatorium all those years," said Morrison, trying his best to be cordial.

Braxton exhaled and focused on his coffee while Morrison continued, "And with the tragedy of our father's passing, it's been a tough year for us."

"I'm gonna stop you there, son..." said Braxton, laying his spoon down on the saucer holding his coffee, then pushing it off to the side in frustration. "Your little dog and pony show you're doing right now isn't fooling anyone, okay? I'm very aware of the contentious relationship you two had with your father, and, let's be honest, I already know that your father didn't care for either one of you. He was a hard, distant man who lived for his work and his research, and you two got lost in the shuffle. I know this. Don't put on pretenses. Just shoot straight with me. You two had him killed, didn't you?"

Both brothers slowly leaned back in the booth, glancing at each other before Morrison responded with, "We don't know what you're talking about."

"You two idiots do realize who I am and who I work for, correct? I have at my disposal the best military police officers and investigators that this country has to offer. You don't think we can look at a crime scene in one of *our* buildings with one of *our* contractors and figure out what really took place? But, for the sake of national security, we don't let sordid details like that come to light, you understand what I'm saying? Sheesh...I think your father was right about you two."

Phillip, Jr. took great exception to the comment, leaning forward in a very hushed, ominous voice and said, "Our father knew nothing about us! He was a fool!"

Braxton looked at the oldest Killiecrankie son, sensing a chilling difference from the young man he had known before. Phillip, Jr. continued, "Our father had a one-track mind. He talked about unlocking the next stages of evolution as if it were something he could just conjure up from thin air in the hopes of manifesting a glorious path of recognition for himself, all the while completely turning a blind eye to real, grounded, scientific advancement. Research that could have real-world effects right now, rather than something that could *possibly* happen in time. Hypotheticals and theories are all he ever had while my brother and I were creating actual scientific advancements that could be used right now. He shunned us despite our efforts, and now he's no more. He was and will always be irrelevant!"

Braxton sat silently, not so much surprised by the lack of denial from the Killiecrankie Brothers over the accusation of involvement in their father's death, but more so by their willingness to implicate themselves out of pure disgust for the man. It was evident the total emotional disconnect and lack of empathy for their actions against their father and the realization of the darkness they held on to told Braxton it would be in his best interest to do whatever he needed in that meeting to keep in their good graces.

"Since your note made mention of a new deal, I'm assuming you were already aware of the military disavowing the original agreement with your father. I don't know what you two think you could possibly offer the military at this point that would be worth our while to enter into another arrangement with your precarious family...no offense."

"What if we told you we have developed a weapon that will put a stop to any war at any time, regardless of army size or scale of escalation?" Morrison asked.

Braxton's brow heightened, and his eyes lit up. He was definitely intrigued.

"That is a very bold claim, young man. If you had such a weapon at your disposal, I'd want to know more details."

Morrison reached into his breast pocket and removed a small notepad.

"My brother and I have been working non-stop for the past six years on a new airborne pathogen that we have been able to pressurize and adapt for military use. Our father always talked about the next big scientific steps. Well, in our opinion, this is it. This pathogen, when introduced into a population, will completely debilitate any and all living things within a designated radius."

"Designated radius? Explain," asked Braxton, becoming more and more interested.

"You can customize the potency of the pathogen, sir," Phillip, Jr. added. "By altering the level of potency, you determine how much area it will cover. You can use it on small dwellings to clear a minor enemy threat or drop it into the middle of a firefight behind enemy lines and knock out hundreds of soldiers within minutes."

"But what about the pathogen getting carried off by wind erosion? Our troops could be caught in a mist of that stuff. What then?"

"The pathogen is engineered with the same characteristics of other dense gases, like carbon dioxide. It's specifically made to disperse and then sink toward the ground. As long as the pressurized capsules are dispersed at an altitude no higher than 150 feet, the pathogen will find its mark. Once the pathogen attaches to an enemy, it begins attacking all living cells. The higher the potency, the deadlier the effects. Once it has run its course, it simply evaporates and you never knew it was there to begin with."

"I must say, gentlemen, I am impressed. Helluva lot better than what your father came up with all those years researching."

The brothers smiled, taking what, realistically, was the first and only compliment for their work they had ever received.

"Of course... something like this has to be backed up with research, notes, and studies before I can get anyone to sign off on it. Where are you two doing your research if the asylum is completely shut down? Sounds like you'd need a pretty big space to do that work."

The brothers didn't say a word, and Braxton immediately picked up on what was going on. "You've been working out of the asylum, haven't you? How?"

"You may have shut down the asylum, Braxton, but the government never disengaged the emergency power systems that bypass local energy sources. So, thanks for keeping the lights on," Phillip, Jr. quipped.

Braxton was not amused but took it in stride.

"And here I thought we left that place in a sorry enough state before we condemned it... guess you boys were able to salvage the old lab, huh?" Braxton said as he took a big swig of his coffee.

Phillip, Jr. glanced at Morrison, and the two brothers had the same thought.

He doesn't know about the secret expansion...

When Phillip, Sr. oversaw the construction of the Sanatorium, he and the major in charge of the program at the time, Major Jasper, had agreed upon a secret expansion to be added to the underside of the building to be used for any number of surprises. State inspections, violent weather, accidental exposure of the secret program. Any one of these was a viable reason for the expansion, and it was approved during construction. What most people who were associated with the program didn't know was that Phillip, Sr., and Major Jasper arranged for that detail to be left out of any planning and schematics, and the laborers for that particular part of the construction were brought in from the military to cut down on civilians being made aware of its existence. So, when Major Jasper was promoted, he passed off the overseeing of the program to newly promoted Major Braxton, who was not made aware of the secret expansion.

"Of course, sir. We're resilient when it comes to our work," said Phillip Jr., going along with the Lt. Col.'s assumptions.

"Test subjects? I'm assuming you have some that you can show some readings from?"

"Of course, of course. Several test subjects," said Morrison, just hoping that he wouldn't ask where they got their test subjects.

"Where did you get the test subjects?" he asked, as if right on cue.

Morrison shifted in his seat and looked to his brother for an assist.

"Volunteers, sir. All volunteers from various facilities. We have paperwork we can show you later," Phillip offered, which was a lie. The reality was the brothers had been using patients from the old regime at the sanatorium as subjects to numerous experimentations by the brothers for the past six years. Fabricated patient files would have to be made up quickly.

Braxton sat in the booth, staring at the table, weighing his options and deeply thinking about the situation at hand. On one hand, he wanted no part of the Killiecrankie name ever again. On the other, if what they offered was legitimate, it would be a game changer for the US Military. The brothers waited in anticipation, not knowing if they had put on a good enough show to sway the veteran military man.

After a long, pregnant pause, Braxton spoke. "Well, guess I'm gonna be making another trip down to that god-forsaken county again. I'm assuming you have regular offices, now, that I can come to this time around? I seem to remember your father going on and on about 'being stabbed in the back' by you two when y'all left his tutelage at the asylum."

Phillip, Jr.'s fists tightened and his teeth clenched. All he could think of was one of the last things his father said to him moments before Phillip, Jr. set into motion the orchestration of his death.

You know what I feel when I look at you? Embarrassment.

Phillip, Jr. took a brief pause, collected himself, and let go of the feelings he had at that moment, plastered on a terrible grin, and said, "Of course we have offices, sir. No need to make the trip out to the asylum. We've got new ways of doing things down in Kentucky, these days."

Braxton stood up from the booth, laid some change on the table to cover the cost of his coffee, and then turned to leave without saying a word. The brothers looked at each other, not fully knowing if he was agreeing to terms or shutting them out.

"So, is that a yes, Lt. Col. Or...?" Morrison asked.

Braxton paused and turned back to the brothers.

"It'll take a couple of weeks, but I'll get my bosses to sign off on it. With so much turmoil overseas these days, anything that'll help the troops will get their full blessing. Off the books, of course. But I'll tell you the same thing I told your father," he said, stepping back toward the booth and tapping his index finger on the table. "You sign on that dotted line, we expect results. Your father never delivered on that...came close one time...that Patient G or H-something or other. Hell, he's probably dead now, too, so it doesn't matter. The point is, you give us results, we give you money. Everyone is happy. Got it?"

The brothers nodded in agreement.

"By the way... you got a name for the weapon?"

"We're calling it Tormerdol," said Phillip, Jr. "Loosely, it means 'Watcher of Pain.'"

The Lt. Col. gave a look of approval and took his leave.

The brothers shook each other's hand and smiled as they got up from the booth and left a few minutes after Braxton. They were more than happy with the outcome of their trip to the nation's capital, but something about the conversation with Lt. Col. Braxton sparked a fury inside Phillip, Jr., and Morrison noticed it right away as they walked down the sidewalk back to their hotel.

"You okay, big brother?" he asked. "Seemed like some things he said in there really got under your skin."

The smile disappeared from Phillip, Jr.'s face.

"He insulted me by speaking about our father in the same breath as us. Now that we have our financial future secured, we need to get back home. I have some built-up hostility, and I know exactly who I want to direct it at."

Chapter Seven
"The Rebirth of Patient H7"

Western Kentucky Rehabilitation and Sanatorium
June 23, 1975, | 10:45 P.M.

The old asylum had been slowly dying on the outside since its condemnation in 1963. The thriving overgrowth of vegetation on the facility grounds had fully consumed the walls of the tall building, claiming it as a trophy for Mother Earth. Virginia Creeper Ivy smothered the gardens and patio areas, slithering up onto the retaining walls like a stalking serpent. In the clear sky above, a bright, full moon shined down, illuminating the entire grounds and highlighting the dilapidated state of the building.

Inside on the main floor in the large entryway, small patches of the roof had broken through and over the years the weather had forced a hole through the ceiling, allowing the moonlight to pierce beyond the disfigured architecture, creating an eerie spotlight on the foyer floor.

In the distance, a car roared down the gravel lane toward the asylum. A light blue, Ford Bronco cut through the overgrown weeds, coming to a dragging stop at the front steps. Opening the driver's side door, Phillip, Jr. hurried toward the entrance, leaving his car door open and the headlights on. At the top of the steps, his brother Morrison appeared in the doorway with a troubled look on his face. As the two met each other, they turned inside and briskly walked through the corridors.

"I thought I told you to keep these patients heavily sedated, brother," snapped Phillip, Jr.

"I *did* have them sedated. It wore off. There's only so much sedative I can give a patient before they go into shock or die! These outbursts have been increasing for weeks, and nothing we're doing is keep them docile. Nothing is working!!" a frantic Morrison Killiecrankie responded, keeping up with his brother as they made their way toward the secret expansion.

There was no power on throughout the main part of the building, and the brothers walked with a single flashlight held by Morrison, illuminating the path ahead. As they entered the maintenance room that leads to the hidden, steel door, their younger brother, Augy, stood prominently off to the side, accompanied by a large group of rough-looking men and women wearing old sanatorium staff uniforms and dirty, tattered doctor's coats. In the center of the room, a collection of oil lanterns was grouped together, casting out a dull, ambient light that dimly lit the faces of the strange people in the room. The rough crew did not look professional in any regard standing there in the maintenance room and had been brought in for much darker purposes.

"All these filthy ex-cons we've brought in to keep the maniacs in check haven't been helping the situations lately either!" he said as he gestured to the group.

A thicker-built man with a tattoo of a pair of aces on his

neck and wearing a ripped-up doctor's coat with dried blood smears stepped toward Morrison, grabbed his arm, then said, "Who the hell you callin' filthy, jackass?"

Phillip, Jr. paused, looking at the incident from across the room. He then looked at his mute, younger brother and said, "Augy, please..."

The big, non-verbal man quickly snagged up the doctor-impersonating convict by the neck with both of his large hands, choking the life from him before snapping his neck like a small stick.

The convict dropped to the ground as the rest of the criminals looked on in quiet disbelief.

Phillip, Jr. slowly turned in a circle, facing each person in the room individually as he turned and said, "You were brought here because society has cast you aside. You are criminals who will always be criminals. Do you think you can do the things you want to do out there?! That's what made you criminals to begin with. But here...we let you act on your urges. We let you *be* criminals. All we ask is you keep your mouths shut and keep the patients in line! AND YOU'RE NOT DOING THAT! I. WANT. ORDER!"

The outburst echoed off the walls. Phillip, Jr. composed himself once again, and then motioned for one of the "staff" to open the false wall, revealing the steel door.

The madness of the corrupt doctor had been building for years. Being firsthand observers of the aggressive and boundary-pushing medical treatments instituted by their father, the brothers learned from an early age what *could* and *could not* be done medically. They also learned what they *should* and *should not* do medically, as well. The dark gray areas of morality and the Hippocratic Oath concerning medical advancement had been exploited many times over throughout the annals of time, and, truth be told, most medical miracles would not be known today without some doctor, somewhere, doing something medically provocative that he should not have.

The theories of "Pain-Induced DNA Evolution" put forth by the eldest Killiecrankie had always fascinated the brothers from an early age. But as the boys grew into men, something inside of both of them shifted, and they only focused on one aspect of the theorem.

"Pain."

Upon reinstating an official partnership with the United States Military, the brothers went straight to work developing thousands of units of Tormerdol to be used in military engagements. After the assassination of President Kennedy and the increased involvement of the United States in the Vietnam Conflict, their deadly pathogen was tapped to be the method by which the United States would win the war and bring their troops home.

Throughout the halls of the Pentagon, it was told that Tormerdol was created by US scientists working off stolen intel from German researchers during the Second World War when in reality, the pathogen was created, bought, and paid for on US soil. The financial freedom that came from their contract with the military allowed the brothers to spend an abundant amount of time implementing a new form of experimentation on the hidden patients in the asylum. Their darkest desires could be fully explored, and the only thing that could hold them back was themselves.

Using the resources they had acquired from the US Military over the next few years, the brothers decided to break ground on a new facility in 1973. Tranquil Meadows Health would serve as a newer, state-of-the-art facility in which the importance of mental health and physical rehabilitation would take center stage while also providing long-term care for elderly citizens. At least, that's what they fed the public.

With their private practices financially hemorrhaging due to mismanagement, the new facility acted as a great front to launder their military resources, taking attention away from their inflated bank accounts versus their failing businesses. Another bonus for the brothers was that the new mental health facility acted as a hunting ground for the doctors, providing new, fresh test subjects to replace the rapidly aging patients hidden away at the asylum. By day, they were upstanding citizens providing much-needed health care. By night, they became the darkest and most heinous of predators the world had ever created.

Unfortunately for the Killiecrankies, the research they had submitted on the pathogen was not only incomplete but, in some cases, results had been fabricated and numbers had been altered to show a more positive output.

Morrison Killiecrankie had been the head of the research for the development of the pathogen, but Phillip, Jr. was the one who took the initiative to use tainted test results and outright fabricated data to ensure that the military stayed interested in their creation.

As it would turn out, the ability to customize the potency for the pathogen was erratic and unpredictable, leading to several instances of friendly-fire deaths. The CIA, however, absolutely loved it, even with its flaws. With the up-tick of covert operations carried out beyond the scope of the military, Tormerdol became the dirty little secret in waging war outside official military parameters.

When the United Nations became suspicious of the elevated death tolls in Southeast Asia unrelated to war efforts in the latter part of the sixties, a secret investigation went underway to determine the cause. Due to the military's efforts to keep the origins of Tormerdol secret, it would take the United Nations investigation years to uncover what was really happening in Southeast Asia. But when they discovered the CIA's abuse of the use of Tormerdol, that's when all the fabricated research came to light.

Phillip had gotten the call from Braxton that afternoon.

"You seem way more amped up than usual, big brother," Morrison observed as he followed his brother down the steel steps leading to the secret section of the asylum. The rest of the "staff" followed down the steps and then fanned out walking past the brothers who had stopped midway down the corridor.

"It's over, brother. It's done." Phillip, Jr. said in an agitated tone.

"What's over?"

"Tormerdol. The contract with the military. Freakin' UN pulled it! They're voting to ban it next week and Braxton told me they already have the votes. It's done!" he replied.

"But, that doesn't mean that the contract has to be done. We can still offer them something else in its place," Morrison said, trying to find a solution that would satisfy the situation.

Phillip, Jr. made a look that told Morrison his brother had already tried something with the Lt. Col., but it didn't work.

"What did you offer him?"

"I told him that we could resume the work that father had worked on."

"YOU WHAT?!" Morrison was incredulous. "Pain Induced DNA Evolution? Is this a joke?! Why would you offer him something we don't have? Father's files on that project are gone; we would have to start all over again!"

"I bluffed, alright. He was on the line, I had nothing, I panicked, and I bluffed, alright? The old SOB saw right through it, then he got pissed."

"Why would he get pissed? What the hell did you say to him?"

"I reminded him of father's work on Patient H7... said that we could resume that treatment... maybe even replicate or improve upon it."

"Oh no. He wasn't supposed to know we still have Patient H7... HE WASN'T SUPPOSED TO KNOW WE HAVE ANY OF THOSE PATIENTS!!" screamed Morrison.

Phillip reached up to his taller brother, slapping him across the face, then grabbed him by his lanky arms.

"CALM DOWN, BROTHER! Listen, without the Tormerdol, we were dead in the water anyway. His finding out we still have H7 changes nothing but the time-line. We will be disavowed, and the military will distance itself from us. There's nothing stopping that. Come tomorrow morning, it will be over. We have until then to clean all this up, and I think you know what that means."

Phillip let go of his brother, and the two stood opposite of each other, locked in a stare-down. After a few tense moments, Morrison exhaled.

"Okay, we still have the new facility, and we still have our practices. We'll funnel whatever money we have left into secured offshore accounts, and we'll deal with the cover story later. We can move a lot of these patients back to Tranquil Meadows tonight. There's plenty of room in the facility and everyone else can be transported to some of the other places we have contacts with in Virginia and Maryland. What do we do about the convicts?"

"We'll tell them to take a hike. They've served their purpose. I doubt any of them will make a fuss after seeing what Augy just did to one of them," Phillip, Jr. said with confidence.

"Sounds like we have a plan, then, big brother. I'll go tell the others," Morrison said as he made his way to the secret expansion.

Phillip, Jr. reached out and stopped his brother.

"Do you have your strap, handy?" Phillip, Jr. asked.

"You know I do, big brother. What did you have in mind?"

"After tonight, you and I won't be able to indulge ourselves like we've been free to do this past decade. I want you to know that I appreciate you, little brother. You've known the darkness inside of me since we were very little, and you've never judged me...not once. You accepted me, and I accepted you, and we've explored this together. I knew it would come to an end at some point, but I didn't want it to. We still have tonight, and there's someone here that I think deserves one final treatment from us."

The expressions on both the Killiecrankie brothers' faces shifted, and through an unspoken feeling, they both turned toward the secret asylum expansion.

Inside the main corridor, the "staff" was assembled and awaiting instructions. Morrison gave instructions as to what to do with the patients as Phillip, Jr., and Augy made their way down the hallway to the right. Halfway down, Phillip, Jr. retrieved a syringe filled with a heavy narcotic from a room full of supplies then continued two doors down to a patient's room with "H7" scratched on the outside of the door.

Inside, the patient who was once a small, frail seven-year-old that Dr. Killiecrankie, Sr. had high hopes for, was now a full-grown man, bound in a straight jacket with multiple sets of shackles attached to his feet. He was awake and fully alert, sitting upright on the floor, facing the door in a manner that would suggest he knew they were coming for him.

The little boy who once upon a time had a sweet, unassuming face had been replaced by a man who had been excessively experimented upon, tortured, and mentally abused.

His face was no longer his own, now covered by a strange metal mask, reminiscent of a gas mask without filters attached to the filter ports. His head was completely void of hair, except for a couple of faint-colored eyebrows and scraggly hairs that still clung to his scalp. Where the hair was missing, in its place, were several metal plates that had been strategically implanted by the brothers directly into Patient H7's brain. Due to the bulk of his frame, an altered straight jacket had been created to ensure his inability to move his arms. Scarred, dirty feet poked out of the bottom of a pair of extremely dingy and aged patient uniform pants. Patient H7 hadn't worn shoes since the day the eldest Killiecrankie had been murdered and, on that day, he was moved to his current room.

In the twelve years since then, Patient H7 had never stepped out of it.

Sounds of commotion and screams could be heard down the corridor as Phillip, Jr. moved into the room, syringe in hand, and injected the narcotic into the neck of Patient H7. He didn't resist. After a few moments, his body went limp. Augy reached down and picked up the bulky patient and carried him over his shoulder out of the room.

At the point where the hallways meet, the scene was chaotic. Patients being beaten and dragged from room to room, "staff" members taking full advantage of the tasks assigned to them, and in the middle of it all stood the 6'7' frame of Morrison Killiecrankie, leather strap in hand, already dripping with blood.

Typically, Morrison would be considered the more "normal" of the three Killiecrankie brothers with boyish good looks and an outgoing personality, but when he held the leather strap in his hand, his entire chemical makeup shifted and the nice-looking man devolved into an evil creation that had an unnatural thirst for pain. He had acquired the nickname "Spanky" from the patients due to his obsession with the leather strap he carried.

No one dared call him that name to his face.

The other two brothers, with Patient H7 laid across Augy's shoulder, approached Morrison in the corridor.

"You ready, little brother?" asked Phillip, Jr.

"I am primed and ready, big brother!" said Morrison, smiling a grotesque smile as the leather strap dangled back and forth with thick, syrupy blood dripping from the end.

"I hope you don't mind but I have something special in mind for H7's final treatment. Give me twenty minutes to set up," said Phillip.

Morrison accepted and went back to doing his dark work.

While Phillip was away setting up, Augy and the "staff" started moving patients from the lower expansion to the main floor into older patient rooms and bundling up the less violent patients into the cafeteria. It was a tedious process, but it was the most effective way to make sure that all patients were accounted for.

After this night, it wouldn't matter if anyone in the public stumbled upon the hidden expansion under the asylum. The

Killiecrankies would be turning the page on this chapter of their life and all evidence of their evil perpetrations would need to be erased from existence.

Nothing could be left to chance.

After about twenty-five minutes, the old lights came back on in the entire facility, flickering and popping, casting light down onto the ruins of the once thriving facility. Morrison was confused as to how and why they were on when Phillip returned with a smile on his face.

"I reconnected the building's central wiring to the military backup power for the lower expansion and flipped the switch. We should have enough power for our final session with Patient H7. Come on." He motioned for his brother to follow.

They went single file down a side corridor, passing their father's old office, around a corner to a familiar hallway. On the left was, Observation Room B, where Dr. Phillip Killiecrankie, Sr. spent many hours with Patient H7. Further down on the right was, Patient Room A6, the room they coordinated their father's death. A poetic story of dark symmetry was being written by the oldest brother.

"It's perfect!" exclaimed Morrison.

After seeing his brother's approval for the tableau, Phillip motioned for him to step into Observation Room B. Toward the back of the room across from the door, strapped to a standing wooden table that was in the shape of an "X", Patient H7 was spread-eagle against the table, arms and legs individually bound by tight straps.

His head drooped, still feeling the effects of the sedative that Phillip, Jr. administered a half hour prior. His straight jacket had been removed to allow for binding to the table, which revealed an additional dozen or so small metal plates surgically implanted into the torso, back, and arms of Patient H7, to which each metal plate had an electrical cord tethered to it that connected across the room to a large, ECT machine that had some intricate, industrial modifications.

Sitting next to that was also a heart rate monitor which was on and showing a steady pulse for Patient H7. On the table, three small, metal vials of Tormerdol sat in a line waiting to be used next to a file folder that was marked "Patient H7-423." Morrison looked at the file folder and gave a slight laugh.

"We're still doing paperwork?" he asked.

Phillip laughed himself, "We're technically still employed by the military till sunrise. Everything has to be in order." The two brothers paused and then let out grotesque laughter.

The scene was indeed horrifying.

After they composed themselves, Phillip opened up the file, made the note, "Final Treatment.," signed his name, and closed the file. He then looked at his brother and said, "Let's begin."

For the next few minutes, the brothers took turns abusing Patient H7. Years of frustration and rage that had built up from discovering who Patient H7 actually was in relation to their father, was coming out full throttle with no sign of holding back. Morrison used the leather strap repeatedly on Patient H7, removing small cuts of flesh from his shoulders and back, while Phillip would alternate the electric shock from the head to the body while also landing punches to the stomach and head.

The assault was absolutely monstrous, and the brothers had worn themselves out in the process, but what was incredible throughout the entire attack was that Patient H7 never once said a word. Never made a sound. Nothing. The heart monitor attached to his chest, remarkably, stayed steady during the entire assault. His sheer will refused to give the brothers the satisfaction of his pain.

They were angered by this.

"Nothing is working on this guy, big brother," said Morrison through heavy breaths. "I want him to scream. I want him to break, but HE GIVES US NOTHING!" Frustrated, he reached back, landing another strike to the chest of Patient H7.

No reaction, just a death stare with dark, empty eyes.

"He's not going to give us anything, Morris. All that he can give we've already taken away from him... except for his mind," Phillip said.

He picked up one of the three vials of Tormerdol and held it up to the face of Patient H7. "Recognize this? Hmm? It's the reason you're wearing that mask, remember? I always imagined that the most satisfying way to watch a man die was to take away his ability to breathe, not just because he loses oxygen, and he gasps for air then dies, no, no. I assumed it was most satisfying because it ultimately takes away the man's ability to think. I can't think of anything more devastating than taking away a man's ability to think."

Patient H7 didn't react. He just kept his dark, empty eyes

staring.

Phillip continued, "I thought for sure using this pathogen was going to kill you the first time I used it on you. Then, I thought it again the second time... then the tenth time... the twentieth, you get the idea! But no! You're still here!!"

Phillip reached forward, connecting the small vial to a port on the side of the mask, pushing the release on the vial, sending the pathogen directly into the mouth and nose of Patient H7. The sudden shock to the system made his head rock back and his body began convulsing. After a few seconds, Phillip reached up and disengaged the mask from Patient H7, revealing the grotesqueness of the rest of his face.   .

His lips had been chewed in sections and calloused back over, and the skin on his nose was irritated bright red from the mask. Blood formed at the base of his nose and started to creep out from the corners of his mouth. The pathogen was doing its dark job.

The mask was an important tool that Morrison had created specifically for Patient H7. Phillip's repeated use of the pathogen as a method of torture had severely damaged the lungs and trachea of Patient H7, even in small doses. They realized that if they wanted to keep him alive, they would need something that would help reintroduce fresh oxygen directly to the damaged internal portions of his body.

The mask became a device that would distribute oxygen via small, surgically installed air ducts that flowed throughout the internal structure of Patient H7's body. He had become a gross science experiment, inside and out, for the amusement of the Killiecrankies.

After a few moments, Phillip placed the mask back onto Patient H7's face who then took in several deep breaths. "The Tormerdol isn't as effective in very small doses without fresh oxygen. And since I've torched your lungs, taking the mask off actually helps you live when introduced to the small dose, but it also kills you because you can't breathe without fresh air from the mask. You see how much fun this is for me?!"

Phillip, Jr. laughed hysterically, tossing the empty vial away into the corner.

"No more messing around, Phil... let's end this now. He is the last biological connection to our father. We get rid of him, we can finally be rid of the old man and this place," Morrison said, still catching his breath.

Patient H7's head was hazy, but his hearing was perfectly fine. *The last biological connection...* That phrase sat awkwardly with the patient, and he closed his eyes.

"What do you mean 'last biological connection'?"

The brothers froze in their tracks, looking at each other. "Who was that?" asked Morrison.

Phillip, Jr. looked through the observation glass out into the hallway toward the corridor. No one was there.

"I don't know... you heard that right?" he asked his brother.

"Hell yes, I heard it! Who was that, Phil?!"

Phillip, Jr. looked out into the hall again, seeing no one. He formed a skeptical look on his face as he turned and stared at Patient H7.

"What did I ever do to warrant your hate?"

Phillip and Morrison stood side by side in disbelief, staring at their prisoner. His eyes were still closed.

"This isn't really happening, is it?" Morrison asked in a weak voice. "It's not possible, right?"

Patient H7's eyes opened wide.

"ANSWER ME!"

The force of the mental demand sent a small shock wave in the room and both brothers stumbled back against the cracked observation window. Stunned, they regained their footing and Phillip, Jr. screamed back, "I HATE YOU BECAUSE YOU WERE BORN!"

He quickly reached out, grabbing the mask off of Patient H7's face, taking away his ability to breathe. He continued into a tirade, "Your very presence in life has been nothing but a harsh reminder to my brother and me how we were never good enough for our father. NEVER! But you, his modern-day medical miracle come along and suddenly he's engaging, and he's spending time with you, lots of time with you. We were pushed aside, never to be noticed ever again. We followed in his footsteps, we studied hard, we earned our way, we became him...AND HE HATED US FOR IT! He gave you more love in his short time with you than he ever gave us, and, for that, I will always despise you. Killing father was satisfying, but killing you...his creation...his precious little laboratory son...ohhhhh, that end will justify all my dark means."

Patient H7 was fighting for his life at this point. The lack of oxygen was shutting down his lungs and his vision was getting blurry. Physically, he was fading fast. Inside, however, he still had enough oxygen to have base-level brain function, and, with his declining energy, he forced out another thought to the brothers.

".....Dr....Killiecrankie... ..was... ..my friend... ..not my father....."

The brothers looked sharply at each other with the realization that Patient H7 didn't know who Dr. Killiecrankie, Sr. was to him. Phillip moved forward and got right in the face of Patient H7,

"You knew right? Come on you had to know. Either our father or the nurse had to have told you, right? Tell me you knew..."

"......knew... ...what?... .....which... ..nurse?....."

Phillip, Jr. let out a maniacal laugh and turned to his brother. "HE DIDN'T KNOW! HE DIDN'T KNOW!"

He turned back to Patient H7, affixing the mask back to his

face. "You're not dying on me just yet. I still have more to take from you! Morris, watch him."

Phillip, Jr. darted out into the hallway and made a sprint back toward the office at the far end of the hall, his old office. Morrison could hear him yelling, "Augy, I need you! Bring two men with you!"

The room fell silent, Morrison standing in a locked stare at Patient H7, who was regaining his strength with fresh oxygen circulating through his body once again.

Their eyes met and Morrison said with a slight laugh, "Telepathy...hmm, incredible. I guess you're the prodigy our dad thought you were all along. Tell me, does it make you sad knowing he's only dead because he loved *you* more than *us*?"

Patient H7 closed his eyes and said,

"....my torment will be your undoing...."

He repeated the line over and over again. Not stopping. The repetitiveness finally got to Morrison who took his strap and hit Patient H7 across the chest.

H7 didn't stop.

Morrison hit him again.

He kept repeating the words.

Morrison began whipping Patient H7 in rhythm with the repeating of the words, neither man backing down.

Patient H7's blood raced from within to the open wounds on his chest and shoulders, cascading down his body and saturating his dingy patient pants while also covering the wiring attached to the metal plates implanted in his chest. The strikes kept coming, but the words never stopped repeating.

Morrison hit him one last time before throwing the blood-soaked leather strap onto the table out of frustration. "WHY WON'T YOU BREAK?!"

Moments later, Phillip Killiecrankie, Jr. returned to the observation room with two "staff" members following closely behind. He looked at his brother, truly feeling the heaviness of the tension in the room. He observed the bloody torso of Patient H7. The wounds were open, and the blood seemed to be flowing at a rapid pace, yet his heart rate readout on the monitor had remained normal during and after the attack.

"Everything okay, little brother?" asked Phillip, Jr..

Morrison just waved him off, catching his breath.

Despite the wounds to his body, the fresh oxygen being taken in by the mask was giving Patient H7 newfound strength. Phillip, Jr. noticed this and quickly tried to bring him down a peg, emotionally.

"I brought some company...hope you don't mind. I see you're more alert now. That's good. I want you to be very alert to what's about to happen. AUGY!!"

Out in the hallway, the large frame of the mute, younger brother slowly passed the cracked observation window and then turned to step into the room. Slumped over his shoulder was the body of a patient wearing a very old and stained gown with a hood wrapped around their head. Augy dropped the patient to the floor with a hard thud, and, from underneath the hood, you heard a breathy gasp followed by a pained moan.

"I couldn't in good conscience let our last encounter in this historic building happen without a going away present for you, but before I give you your gift, I want to tell you a couple of things. First, I know it's you who has been riling up the other patients and getting them to fight back against my staff. Your clever little mind trick is very impressive, but you've run out of time to rally your troops. Sorry, about that. But, I'll be sure and take really good care of all of them when we're done here. Second, our father may have discovered you can do a little telepathy, and he may have even told you that you were special. You probably believed him, too, but the reality is he only kept you around because he had to. You came out of a cheap nurse he was messing around with while our sweet mother lie dying at home. You, think he wanted you? He didn't even give you a name!"

"None of this is true... You're just trying to punish me differently because you know you can't break me... YOU CAN'T WIN!!"

The lights in the observation room flickered slightly. Phillip reached over and turned on the modified ECT machine which kickstarted a heavy hum that vibrated on the floor. The meters registered steady in the middle, and then he flipped a small switch sending current into Patient H7's body.

The brothers had never used this technique before on *all* of the metal plates at the same time. They would mainly focus on sending the current directly to the plates implanted in the head at a much lower voltage and only in short bursts. Their goal had always been to torture Patient H7 to satisfy their dark urges, but on this night, their goal was to end Patient H7.

The current hit hard at first, then steadied out. The blood that had been running down his torso from the open wounds seemingly stopped flowing, hovering in place on his body like bloody icicles.

"You're absolutely right, I am punishing you. But you're wrong about the doctor. Our dad was also your dad, and I killed him for it. He fathered you with one of the nurses from this very building. Don't believe me? Just ask her."

Phillip reached over and removed the hood from the patient lying on the floor.

It was Nurse Rucker. She was still alive!

".....You?... ..You were my friend... but you're... are you?... Are you what they say you are??"

Phillip raised the dial on the machine another notch, sending another wave of electricity through the metal plates on Patient H7's body. The blood that was on the metal plates arced an electrical surge to the wiring, causing a series of sparks that everyone in the room shielded their eyes from.

Augy picked up Nurse Rucker, who was very weak from years of abuse and held her facing Patient H7. She looked at the man who was once a scared little boy who clung to her out of instinct, not knowing she was his real mother. She cried as she looked at him, seeing what cruel fate the brothers had dealt her son, knowing that for the early part of his life, she, too, was responsible for what he had become. She looked at him, knowing that they didn't have much time left, but she took full advantage of it.

"I'm so sorry, son...for everything. You didn't ask for any of this and I'm so sorry, but don't you dare listen to these pathetic men. You hear me?! Your father believed in you, more than he ever believed in these disappointments!"

Morrison picked up the leather strap and whipped the nurse across her back, knocking her loose from Augy's heavy grip and, dropping her to the ground.

Augy quickly picked Nurse Rucker up from the floor, holding her in front of her son again.

Patient H7's eyes widened, dark as a moonless night.

With bloody tears running down her face, she spoke to her son.

"Don't forget that you are special, son. These cowards lied to you. Your father did give you a name. Your name is-"

Phillip, Jr. removed a large knife from his waistband slitting the throat of the nurse before she could say Patient H7's name.

The nurse fell to the ground, gasping for air and holding her hands around the wound as her blood poured out onto the floor.

Without hesitating, Phillip, Jr. grabbed the two remaining

metal vials of Tormerdol, standing directly in front of Patient H7, then said, "Let's see how satisfying it is to watch you die!" He then jammed both vials into the ports on either side of the mask and injected the pathogen into Patient H7's mouth and nose. Phillip turned away, grabbed the large dial on the ECT machine, and cranked it to the highest setting possible.

The electric spark that shot out of Patient H7 triggered a seismic pulse that rocked the foundation of the entire facility and even stretched out beyond the property of the old asylum. Farmhouses and residential homes nearby experienced foundational tremors and electrical disturbances.

Inside the asylum, down the corridors, the patients who had been brought up from the secret expansion from transport started to howl and cry and scream as loud as they could in the old patient rooms and offices they had been locked in.

The entire electrical system of the backup military power sources back-loaded the charge and then immediately shot it back out in a dazzling display of sparks, blown circuits, and exploding light bulbs. Every room in the run-down facility became a spectacular light show of electrified energy that filtered out onto the overgrown grounds under the full moon sky.

Back in the observation room, the Killiecrankie brothers watched as Patient H7 was being electrocuted to death while simultaneously being burned from the inside of his body by the Tormerdol. They had created the most horrific way for the rejected half-brother to perish. Or so they thought.

What the Killiecrankie brothers didn't realize they were

doing was just an extreme version of their father's original work: "Pain-Induced DNA Evolution." Their father had already unlocked the initial phases of the DNA code in Patient H7 through similar treatments that were not as advanced as the younger Killiecrankie's torture methods.

Early testing had revealed the special attributes of the young patient's electrically-charged blood he had inherited from his mother that helped send more signals to the brain and generate faster blood flow. The heart can only introduce so much new blood with fresh oxygen to the system, but, because of surgical alterations made to Patient H7's internal system, as long as he's wearing the mask, an infinite amount of pure oxygen is always introduced directly to his blood, bypassing the filtration through the heart, which meant hyper-advanced brain function and higher use of internal brain mapping.

The real innovation, unbeknownst to the brothers, was the metal plates that were surgically attached to the body and skull. These metal plates acted as an electrical road map that rapidly transmitted electrical current through the genetic electrical markers in his blood, altering the dynamics of his blood flow. What was once erratic cell activity became uniformly, synchronized harmony of the blood. Instead of attacking the internal body tissue after being electrically charged, looking for an escape, the blood became compliant with the orders given by the brain and followed the electrical path of the metal plates, looping constantly in a Mobius strip of infinite, recharging energy, boosting Patient H7's telepathy and healing.

Another thing that was occurring that was of great

scientific and biological note was that Patient H7's DNA began to rewrite its own code based on the trauma it was experiencing. When the double dose of Tormerdol was introduced after the ECT machine had been, electrically speaking, "jump-starting his blood," the blood cells didn't try to escape the trauma and pain like when Patient H7 was younger. Instead, the blood cells recognized the pathogen as an enemy and began sending rapid electrical pulses throughout the body, bouncing from blood cell to blood cell, mobilizing the cells to act as a military surgical strike that targeted the Tormerdol pathogen, eradicating it.

The phenomenon created quite a visual with the blood that had run from his wounds. Defying gravity and holding steadily in place, electrical surges arced to the seemingly frozen-in-place blood, causing it to flow back into Patient H7's body.

"Pain-Induced DNA Evolution" wasn't just theorized around the notion of physical pain. Emotional pain was also considered to be a possible catalyst for unlocking a subject's abilities.

Phillip Killiecrankie, Sr. never gave it much thought in his early research but changed his outlook on the theory when he met Nurse Rucker. She brought a more delicate, human approach to the research that he had never quite comprehended. She showed him that human evolution wasn't strictly based on physical attributes and that matters of the heart could also affect matters of the body and mind. When they agreed to conceive a child for research purposes, he finally understood what she meant the first time he observed her holding their son. He couldn't fully feel the emotion, but he could surely see the excitement she felt as a new mother. Based on that, he shifted his approach and came up with a new theory: "Physical pain can unlock special abilities while emotional pain can strengthen them."

However, the seven-year-old boy was too young to understand how to process his emotions when his favorite nurse went away and his friend, Dr. Killiecrankie, was killed, never to be seen again. So, he crawled into a dark hole within himself, forgetting his abilities, and taking on the torment from his captors, until one day, the physical pain reminded him of what he could do. He started to push back in his mind, speaking to the other patients in the asylum through his thoughts. Encouraging them to fight back as well! Waiting for the right opportunity to fulfill a vow he made to himself to finally free himself of this prison. A prison that was all he ever knew. And now, this night, he would take his opportunity to be reborn!

He looked at his dying mother on the ground before him, and the emotional pain triggered a rage within him that would alter the course of his dark storyline forever.

From deep within, a guttural cry started low and then slowly rose into a steady roar.

"...oooorrrrrrrrrrrrrrrrrrrraaaaaaaaaaahhhhhhhhhhhhhh hhhhhhhhhhhhhhhhhhhhhhhhhhhhhh!"

The sound was deafening inside the minds of the three Killiecrankie brothers and their "staff" members. They held their heads in their hands, screaming violently, as the sharp noise from inside sliced through their brains and vibrated all of their senses.

In a quick moment, all the bindings that held Patient H7 tightly to the wooden table, snapped like weak rubber bands, finally freeing him from his torturous state. He took one step forward, ripping off all the wires from the ECT machine that connected to his metal plates, holding them tightly in his hand with the machine still sending a steady current.

One of the "staff" members, with a hammer in his hand, made a move toward Patient H7, who quickly grabbed him by the throat and then shoved the electrical wires from the ECT machine into his eyes, sending the abnormally high electrical current directly into this eyes and brain.

As he fell to the ground, the second "staffer" had already stepped forward swinging a block of wood with nails driven through the end, creating a crude version of a mace.

Patient H7 ducked the attacker, reached up to his shoulder, and removed one of his implanted metal plates, revealing a 3-inch spike on the end which he immediately used to stab the attacker in the neck. He twisted it in place, then yanked it back out and proceeded to re-implant the plate back into his shoulder.

Morrison Killiecrankie, who was still reeling from the initial scream from within, watched in horror as his victim became the attacker. He pushed his older brother against the cracked observation room window and made a quick attempt for the door but just as he hit the threshold, Patient H7 extended his hand in front of him and made a swipe motion with his fingers, using his mind to slam the door onto Morrison's "leather strap holding" hand, who shrieked in pain.

His abilities had rapidly evolved, and the older Killiecrankie brother panicked.

Phillip. Jr, raised his knife above his head as he darted straight at Patient H7, who flicked his fingers, making the knife fly out of Phillip's hands and embedding into the far wall.

Patient H7 opened his hand and widened his fingers, using his newfound telekinetic abilities to pull Phillip, Jr. into a tight choke hold. Patient H7 raised his other hand and pulled Morrison in from the doorway, making the 6'7" half-brother come down to a lower elevation while he towered above them both. His grip tightened and his dark eyes peered out over the mask that covered his face, staring at the brothers.

"My torment will be your undoing!!"

Patient H7's grip intensified while the brothers began to shake and convulse from loss of oxygen. The sight made Patient H7 laugh, only the laughter was inside their heads, creating a nightmarish soundtrack for their demise. H7 was just about to succeed in his retribution when a large fist came crashing into his periphery, smashing the left side of his face and sending him careening against the back wall.

Auguste Killiecrankie had, for the time being, saved his brothers from the clutches of their half-brother.

Quickly catching their breath, the older brothers seized the opportunity to escape, darting for the door.

"Augy, finish him off and take the service truck back to town. Forget about the patients! Phillip, Jr. barked out the order to his mute brother as he and Morrison made a quick getaway from the observation room.

Patient H7 had recovered at this point, and when Augy turned to continue his attack, Patient H7 raised both hands, lifting the massive brother off the ground and pulling him from across the room. Augy's eyes opened wide, and his face went as white as a sheet as he landed in the amazingly strong arms of Patient H7.

"I know you can't talk... but you can hear... so hear this now... tonight... you all die!"

Patient H7 lifted Augy above his head and hurled him across the room, crashing through the window on the opposite side of the door and landing hard against the wall across from Observation Room B.

Patient H7 slowly and methodically made his way across the room intending to finish off Augy before heading after the other brothers, but before he could make it to the doorway, a slight whisper echoed inside his mind.

"Son..."

He stood still, turning to look at Nurse Rucker, his dying mother, lying on the ground with her hand still weakly applied to her mortal wound. The last bit of oxygen coursed through her body by the same blood cell traits she passed to her son. The final sparks of electrical charge from her blood sent the last signals to her brain that she would ever transmit.

She felt fortunate to be with him, at that moment, regardless of the short time she had left. He knelt beside her, touching her other hand that clumsily laid across her stomach. Her skin was cold and pale. It wouldn't be much longer now.

"Please stay with me..."

Outside in the hall, Augy had gotten back to his feet and was limping toward the entrance. He paused at the door, only briefly, then continued, wanting no more of the superior strength of Patient H7.

"I'll stay with you..."

"It'll be over soon, son..."

"I know...."

"Life is full of pain... but also full of hope... you'll have to find your own way through both..."

"............"

"New Hampshire... find him..."

"What?! Find who?!"

"...I... I... "

"You what? What are you trying to tell me?!"

"..............."

Abigail Rucker succumbed to her injuries right there on the floor of the same room she had spent so many hours with Patient H7 in his early years. During those days, she was only Nurse Rucker, Patient H7's best friend in the little world he made for himself behind the walls of the asylum.

On this night, however, she had gotten to be a mom to her son for the first and only time. Patient H7 grabbed a patient's gown that was lying nearby and covered his mother's body. He paused for a split second, stood up, and closed his eyes, taking in a long, slow, deep breath.

He exhaled, opened his eyes, and then spoke out into the void...

"Kill them all!"

Chapter Eight
"The Fall of the Asylum"

Henderson County Sheriff's Office
June 24, 1975 | 12:17 A.M.

Deputy Martin sat in the lounge at the Sheriff's Office with his legs crossed and resting on a short coffee table, listening to a local country music station. He had drawn the short stick for the graveyard shift that night, and after about his third cup of coffee and his fourth updated file, he had completely run out of things to do. He wasn't about to complain about being on call for the evening with nothing to do, having just recently made the switch from the Henderson City Police Department where patrols could get a little dicey in rougher parts of town.

He had posted a very honorable career with the city for over a decade and decided to make the change to the deputy in the hopes it would be a slower change of pace. The newly elected Sheriff Dobson was highly respected in the county and Deputy Martin was eager and ready to work under his guidance.

The deputy stood up and made his way down a hallway with only one light on and entered the bathroom. When he had finished and stepped back out into the hallway, he could hear the radio for 911 dispatch scratching in a call. He yawned, walking back toward the sound, assuming it was another call about some drunk at a bar who had made a scene or a rowdy couple getting into an argument that was too loud for the neighbors. Martin picked up the receiver and answered.

"Deputy Martin, go ahead..."

"Sir, we are getting calls from all over the east end of the county with noise complaints, power surges, and some callers saying it felt like a bomb went off. Over."

He closed his eyes and sighed heavily. *This always happens...* he thought to himself.

"Well, did you tell them it was probably just some idiot kids lighting off Cherry Bombs? Over."

"Negative, sir, We are still getting calls from dozens of people saying it sounds like there's something going on at the old asylum. We need you to go investigate, please. Over."

"Clara, if you're messing with me again, I swear...'"

"Not messing with you, sir. We're up to twenty-three calls. Over."

Twenty-three? he thought to himself. *That's an abnormal amount of calls just for hooligan kids.*

"10-4, copy that. I'm headed that way, now. Over."

"Copy."

Deputy Martin hung up the radio receiver, grabbed his deputy's hat from the table, and headed outside to his car. Within minutes, he was cruising down Highway 60 in the direction of the old sanatorium. Growing up in the area, Deputy Martin was certainly aware of the horror stories of the old asylum.

According to all the legends he had heard, Dr. Killiecrankie was a mad scientist who would use his patients as guinea pigs for weird, new drugs and when they resisted, he would surgically alter them, turning the patients into horribly disfigured monsters that he would then let run free around the county on full- moon nights, and then, one night, they turned on him, killing him and eating his body!

He naturally thought all the stories were absolute BS and would get highly irritated anytime they were brought up. Ghost stories were for kids.

Deputy Martin gazed out through the windshield, staring out at the night with the full moon overhead revealing the county's shaded landscape. Aside from his patrol car and a light blue Ford Bronco that whipped past him heading back toward town, the countryside seemed to be petrified into stillness. The proverbial deer in the moon headlight. The deputy liked the peace of that visual.

As he drove, he kept thinking to himself, *There better not be another group of kids out past curfew doing stupid stuff near the asylum,* and he also thought, *If Clara tricked me into driving all the way out to that damn asylum again, I will never hear the end of it from the other deputies.*

He was zoned out for a bit, lost in thought when a most peculiar sight in the road up ahead broke his trance.

"What in the blue hell is that?!" he said out loud to himself.

In the opposite lane, about fifty yards ahead, a man was running in a dead sprint, wearing a white lab coat. Behind him, fast on his heels, was a woman in a grayish patient's gown. As Martin got closer, he flipped on his emergency lights and slowed the car down to see better. As he did, the woman in the gown jumped onto the back of the man in the lab coat, wrapping her arms around his head.

Deputy Martin, stunned, slammed on his brakes and got out of the car, drawing and aiming his weapon at the woman. He yelled for her to stop and let go of the man, but she ignored his commands. Her arms squeezed tight around the man's head and neck as he fought to get up from the ground. The woman wasn't saying a word, but the man was screaming muffled screams from under the pressure of her arms.

Deputy Martin ordered the woman to stop, who ignored him again and kept on with her assault. He holstered his firearm and made a run for the woman, trying to separate her from the man on the ground. As Martin grabbed her torso, she quickly wrenched her arms, snapping the man's neck and letting his head drop onto the asphalt. The sound of the break seemed amplified in the still of the county air on that dark stretch of Highway 60.

Deputy Martin quickly got back to his feet, in complete shock, re-drawing his firearm and aiming it at the crazed woman again, only this time, she did not resist. She stood perfectly still, staring at the deputy, revealing a severely burned right side of her face. He ordered her to the ground, which she complied with, and he quickly cuffed her and placed her in the back of the patrol car.

Once he knew he was safe from her, he exhaled heavily and began to panic.

"Oh my God, oh my God…" he repeated to himself,

staring at the dead man in the lab coat on the ground.

He reached inside the patrol car, grabbed his radio receiver, and sent out a distress call for immediate backup and EMS. After dispatch confirmed his request, Deputy Martin took a second to catch his breath.

He walked to his trunk, removing a road hazard flare, igniting it, and laying it in the road about twenty yards behind him. Then another one ten yards closer. Then another one on the other side of the accident. He came back to where the assault occurred and knelt down to shift the body of the dead man in the lab coat out of the road. When he rolled the corpse over onto its back, he stood back up in a confused state, staring down at the dead face that was staring back at him.

"Ronnie McElroy?" he questioned.

"Why the hell would a no good arsonist be in a lab coat in the middle of the night?" he asked himself. He turned and faced the woman with the burned face in the back of the patrol car, who looked at him through the glass, smiling.

Ronnie McElroy had been arrested several times in Henderson County on many different counts of arson and attempted murder before he just up and vanished three years prior. The last arresting officer in his file was Deputy Martin who had told the fire-obsessed felon that if he ever caught him attempting to burn another person ever again, he wouldn't waste his time arresting him; he'd just shoot him.

That threat got Ronnie's charges dropped, and he was set free. Until this night, no one had seen or heard from the convict and now he lay dead on the side of the road, strangled, and neck snapped by a woman that, as far as Deputy Martin could tell, had been another victim of Ronnie's obsession.

Good riddance, the deputy thought.

Then suddenly, Deputy Martin could hear a faint noise in the distance. He focused his hearing, trying to block out the ambient noise of night so that he could make out the noise. It was getting louder but still too obscure. He took a second to figure out where he was and where exactly the noise might be coming from. Then the stark realization hit him hard. It was screams, and they were coming from the direction of the asylum.

He stood still for a brief moment, frozen in place, not knowing what he should do. Then a sense of service and duty took over, and he got back into his patrol car, grabbing the radio. He called out again for help and backup and was told that EMS and other deputies were only minutes out. In his rearview mirror, he could see the faint police lights making their way down the highway in his direction, but then his focus shifted to the face of the burned woman in the back seat.

"Miss…what happened to you tonight? Can you tell me how you got here?"

"His torment will be their undoing…we must kill them all…"

She repeated the words over and over again, in a low, soft voice while staring in a trance as if she had been possessed by another entity. Deputy Martin made another attempt to talk, but the girl just kept repeating the same words. He knew there wasn't anything he could get from the girl, so he left her alone to her words in the back seat.

The backup was now within a few hundred yards, and Deputy Martin got on the radio to say he was going to make his way down the private lane to the asylum, also alerting EMS to the deceased felon on the side of the road. He shifted the car into drive and made for the asylum.

Driving down the overgrown lane with the monstrous-looking oaks and maples hovering overhead, the headlights made dancing shadow figures that crept in and out of the trees in a hellish light show. Deputy Martin was on edge from before with the encounter on the highway and now he was on very high alert for what lay beyond the tree line. The screams he heard before from the highway were like shrieking banshees now as he passed the clearing and came face-to-face with the old asylum, that stood tall and backlit by the moon.

He stopped the car, and, in front of him, his headlights showcased a vile, chaotic scene that would scar a permanent spot in his psyche for the rest of his days.

A flood of men and women dressed as patients spewed from the broken-down entryway of the condemned asylum, spilling out into the overgrown wraparound driveway and adjoining courtyards, stalking another larger group of men and women who were dressed as hospital staff. Doctor's jackets, lab coats, surgical gowns, and the entire hospital wardrobe were on display and being eviscerated by the group dressed in patient gowns.

Those dressed as staff were fighting off those dressed as patients, screaming for help and for their lives as some of the patients got their hands on a couple of those unfortunate souls. So much violence was being inflicted there under the moonlight, with blood spilling onto the ground in a macabre river of death. The patients did unspeakable things to the people dressed as staff, who were breaking away and running off in different directions, trying to escape their attackers.

Some tried to make a run for the side courtyard that led out to the wheat field meadow. Others found themselves pinned down between the east wall and the tree line. A handful broke free, sprinting for the woods beyond the meadow, only to be tracked down by the tenacious patients.

Their final screams echoed through the woods.

The young girl in the back kept repeating her words, but now she was rocking back and forth and would occasionally hop up and down on the seat. Deputy Martin sat in the front seat, watching the dark play of violence act out before him, completely helpless as to what to do.

If he were to engage this crowd, he would certainly find himself on the losing end rather quickly. He had no choice but to wait until the sheriff and the other deputies would arrive.

It took a full two minutes and during that time, Deputy Martin witnessed several deaths, one of which happened on the hood of his car when two of the patients caught up to a stocky, fleeing man, wearing a blood-stained apron, slamming him onto the hood. He appeared to be a kitchen staff person of sorts, wearing garb that perhaps a butcher would wear. One patient proceeded to beat him with a kitchen rolling pin while the other took a large butcher's cleaver and slammed it down into the center of his chest, leaving him writhing and choking on his blood before he stopped moving and bled out.

During the two minutes of extended chaos, Deputy Martin also noticed a man with a large build, walking with a noticeable limp, leaving from a small doorway on the west side of the building, moving as quickly as he could with the injury toward the long tree line on the other side of the meadow. He also noted that the injured man successfully fought off a couple of the patient attackers in the middle of the meadow before disappearing into the darkness of the forest. Soon after, another man emerged from the building, wearing only a pair of pants, and following after the large, limping man toward the woods. This second man walked much slower and took his time, before disappearing into the forest, as well. He couldn't tell any distinguishing characteristics of either man, due to being so far away, but one thing was for sure, they were both large men.

At this time, several of the patients turned their attention toward Deputy Martin's car and started pushing the patrol car side to side while attempting to smash open the windows. The young girl was in the back bouncing off the seats into the doors and then back onto the seat, clapping and hollering loudly.

Martin couldn't sit here any longer, he was going to have to drive his way out, but just then, in his rearview mirror, he saw the flashing lights of backup. Several vehicles pulled onto the scene, and deputies quickly hopped out and took defensive positions with their weapons drawn.

Surprisingly, a good number of the people dressed as patients complied with officers when instructed to surrender; however, there were also an equal number of those who did not comply. While trying to apprehend those who were dressed as patients, there was still a handful of the group of people dressed as staffers who were begging the police to save them. Almost all of these people were immediately recognized as ex-cons and felons by the officers on the scene, which added another layer of chaos and confusion to an already combustible situation.

With the elevated police presence on the scene, Deputy Martin felt comfortable enough to exit his vehicle and begin helping control the scene. Newly-elected Sheriff Dobson connected with his deputy in the fringes of the chaos.

"Do we have any idea what the hell is going on here, deputy?!" Dobson yelled, followed by tackling a patient to the ground and cuffing him.

"I haven't the faintest damn clue, sir. Something is horribly wrong here!"

The crew of deputies worked together to try and wrangle up all the various people at the scene. There was no way of telling who was good or bad or otherwise. The entire scene was nothing but destruction and chaos. Bodies lie beaten and battered, blood spattered on every possible surface, and throughout the overgrown land in front of the old building, dozens of people dressed as patients wandered about, oblivious to the commanding officers standing before them.

A few patients made moves toward the deputies, who then

fired warning shots into the country air, hoping to dissuade them from advancing. This sent a shock through the rest of the mass of people who then fled for cover back inside the old, broken-down asylum.

Sheriff Dobson and Deputy Martin led the officers to the front of the building, who then made their way inside, performing a security sweep, moving from room to room. They began rounding up patients who, once they realized that the police weren't there to hurt them, peacefully complied with the officer's commands and surrendered.

The scene inside was surreal. Dead bodies lie atop dead bodies with pools of blood on every possible surface. The corridors stunk of fresh blood and most of the deputies had to cover their faces from the stench.

As the officers made their way through the labyrinth of offices and old patient rooms, old pictures of doctors and staff members from a time gone by were lying in messy angles on the floor. The eyes of all of the old staff members were scratched out and replaced with dripping blood. Medical equipment was caked with blood and body tissue, a total forensics nightmare. The condition of the facility was horrendous and soon, the questions among the deputies started swirling as to who these people were and why were they there.

Sheriff Dobson and Deputy Martin stayed close to each other as the sweeps continued from corridor to corridor. As they stepped into a back hallway, they heard loud shuffling and then the sound of a door slamming. Both men followed the sound to a storage room that had an exterior door. They carefully opened the door, checking to make sure no one was going to get the drop on them.

Once outside, the officers carefully looked around and saw no one. Deputy Martin looked at the positioning of the door and recognized it as the door where the large limping man exited from. Sheriff Dobson recognized it as the door he made entry into when he stumbled upon the gruesome discovery of Dr. Phillip Killiecrankie, Sr.'s body.

This night would prove to be far more heinous.

"Whatever we heard definitely came out this way into the meadow. You see anything?" asked Dobson.

"I don't sir, ...but I think whoever it was went toward that tree line," said Deputy Martin, pointing toward a space between two massive oaks on the edge of the meadow.

Dobson double-checked his pistol, making sure he had full funds, to which Martin followed suit.

"Let's go then, deputy," Dobson said as he turned and made his way toward the tree line.

After passing the threshold between the forest and the meadow, an odd silence befell the forest floor as the two officers slowly navigated the dark shadows. The moonlight danced within the leaves of the overhead trees, sending weird light patterns bouncing off the barks and branches. Sheriff Dobson maintained a visual to his front while Deputy Martin slowly walked backward keeping a visual behind.

After about thirty yards, Dobson spotted a torn piece of cloth from a medical gown clinging to a sticker bush at the base of a Catalpa tree. Without saying a word, he showed it to Martin and then motioned to keep pressing forward. They continued following what seemed like a pseudo-foot path that they could see would open up to a clearing about forty yards away. In the distance, both men heard a sound, and they came to a halt, focusing in on the sound. It was the heavy hum of a truck.

Someone was escaping!

They both dropped into a sprint, guns still in their hands as they approached the clearing up ahead, revealing a dirty, grass-patched county road. The heavy hum had become silent, and the truck was gone. Someone had arranged for safe passage away from this place and along with them, they took an explanation for the monstrous chaos that took place only a few hundred yards away.

The officers dejected, turned to make their way back through the forest to the "crime scene of the century" when something caught their eyes on the edge of the dirty, grass-patched road.

They both drew their guns and approached slowly.

On the ground, a large man with a huge scar on top of his head that ran from the back to his hairline was dead from a series of horrific bone breaks and a large gash in his forehead. His body was contorted and grotesque, and his eyes were lifeless and fixated in a forward stare. Sheriff Dobson rolled him onto his back, revealing a dingy, stained name patch affixed to a service uniform that read "Augy."

"You recognize him?" asked Dobson.

"Aside from seeing him escape out the side door of the asylum, I don't, sir. A man this big I think I would probably remember, but he ain't ringing' any bells." Deputy Martin replied.

Dobson took a deep breath. "This is going to take weeks to process."

Sheriff Dobson's radio crackled on his belt. "*Sheriff Dobson, come back.*"

"Go ahead, deputy."

"*Whatever you're doing, you need to stop and get back here to the asylum. We've found something.*"

"What is it?"

"*You just need to see it for yourself.*"

Dobson and Martin looked at each other, not sure what awaited them upon their return to the asylum and not fully sure they wanted to know. They kept their guns drawn and held up their flashlights as they began the long walk back to the scene of the dark, violent play that had just taken center stage.

Chapter Nine
"The Philosopher"

Outside the residence of Morrison Killiecrankie

July 21, 1986 | 8:35 P.M.

The afternoon sky gave way to the darkness of space with a visual grudge match taking place out on the horizon where light and dark battled each other, every morning and afternoon. An atmospheric wonder was occurring in the sky with blazing shades of yellow, orange, and red, fading into the calm feelings of violets, purples, and dark blues. The Kentucky air was still a bit warm, but it was manageable. There wasn't a cloud in the sky, and the back-lit canvas of the nighttime projected out the twinkling of stars in a dazzling, stationary light show.

The other light show was the sea of police and ambulance lights spinning their frenetic displays of reds, blues, and whites off the nearby neighborhood homes. The street in front of Morrison Killiecrankie's home had morphed into a chaotic wave of erratically parked police vehicles which had dwindled in numbers over the past few hours as officers were dismissed from the scene to return to their normal patrols.

The apparent torture and murder of the local doctor would surely bring up many feelings in the community once the news outlets had picked up on the story. Police officers investigating the scene could already envision the potential headlines by clever newspaper editors, with no scruples or morals, looking to sell an extra paper.

"DOCTOR'S HOUSE CALL TURNED DEADLY!"

"A CASE OF BAD MEDICINE!"

"LIKE FATHER, LIKE SON."

The investigation by the detectives of the Henderson Police Department drudged on as nighttime fell. Occurring within city limits and the victim being a city resident, the HPD predictably asserted their jurisdiction over the case once on scene. They "politely" asked that the sheriff, his deputies, and SA Whittaker remain close by for any follow-up questions they may have.

Considering everything that had happened during this full-day, Sheriff Dobson was more than happy to allow the city police to handle the investigation. This allowed him some time to fully catch up with Whittaker with the timeline regarding exactly what had happened at the asylum in 1975.

When Dobson had finished with his recounting of the night, they discovered what had become of the missing patients, Whittaker and Harkins, both, were flabbergasted.

"It was the hidden expansion of the sanatorium, wasn't it? What your deputy radioed to you that night as you were discovering the dead body on the county lane…your deputies found the expansion and all its secrets?"

"That's affirmative, Special Agent. So many dead bodies. So much blood. I can't even begin to describe the carnage left behind in that damn broken-down building that night." Dobson said, looking away in disgust as he recalled the visuals.

He took a beat, then turned back and said, "That wasn't all they discovered that night, down in the expansion, that is. There was something else."

Whittaker perked up. "There was a second lab down there. Inside were all sorts of notes and files pertaining to chemical testing that had been thrown about. One file folder stood out among the scattered notes with the word 'Tormerdol' stamped on the front." Whittaker's eyes lit up in shock.

"Tell me you still have that file." Dobson shook his head.

"The file was empty. Someone had taken the contents. Believe me, I checked the floor and all the other pages tossed about on the floor." Whittaker was deflated.

"There was, however, a crate on the floor in the back corner of the lab that still had a sizable amount of cartridges that we assumed had the deadly pathogen. Not wanting to accidentally trigger a chemical catastrophe, I told my deputies to leave it there, and we'd handle it later. The military seized all of it rather quickly which told me their real motives for scrambling so fast to keep everything pretty quiet."

"And I'm guessing Colonel Braxton also made it abundantly clear that 'as a man who displays a shield on his chest, that it was your civic duty to keep this quiet due to 'National Security' right?"

Whittaker asked with a purely sarcastic tone that made him sick just saying it out loud.

"It's like you were there in the room during the discussion," Dobson said with a joking tone.

His demeanor was comparable to that of a man who had started to feel truly free of a life-altering burden

"What you're telling me is pure insanity... you realize that, don't you? None of this makes any sense in logical thought," said Whittaker.

"In a million years, I never woulda' believed it... but it's real. Saw the whole damn thing with my own eyes... and it's stayed with me every day since then," Martin added, reiterating the severity of the situation. "Every missing person, every dead body that turns up, it reminds me of that night. Most times I can't shake it."

"I don't even know how to react to that, partner," Harkins said, reaching out and patting Martin on the arm.

The former military man had a very frustrated look on his face. "I can't believe our US Military and our own government would do such a thing... a cover-up? That's lying directly to the faces of our citizens, and putting you in that position, sir, all these years later...it's just not right, sir," he angrily said, talking directly to Sheriff Dobson, a man he respected and admired very much.

"I appreciate that, son, but right now, what they did back then doesn't matter. What matters now is what our next steps are going to be. Whittaker was right earlier today when he said that whoever is behind this has a story they want to tell. "*Sins will soon be on display...*" Who is putting on the show?" asked Dobson, looking to his deputies and SA Whittaker for any theories or ideas for leads.

"Well, I overheard the detectives saying that the two men I engaged with during the encounter don't match the descriptions of any missing patients from any nearby hospitals or wellness facilities, and they don't have any apparent ties to Morrison Killiecrankie. Is it possible they're from out of state, and we *are* dealing with some kind of cult that might be the connection between Colonel Braxton and Morrison Killiecrankie?" asked Harkins.

"*...heh heh heh ha ha ha ha hahahaha....*"

The laughter boiled up fast and came out of nowhere from the back of Whittaker's mind. The sudden onset showed on his face through a slight grimace and Sheriff Dobson took notice.

"I don't think we're dealing with a cult, exactly. Whoever is behind all this is manipulating situations and people to give him the positioning to deliver his message. It's not about the message, singularly... it's about the *display* of the message."

"*...The Philosopher is right again!....*"

"Oh, god!" Whittaker shrieked before covering his mouth,

drawing the looks of a couple of city police officers across the yard who immediately lost interest and went back to their conversations. The pain from the voice in the void was way more intense than any other time before. He sat down on the bumper of the patrol car, taking a huge breath of air.

"You alright, Special Agent?" asked Dobson, knowing the answer but giving Whittaker the chance to either lie or tell the truth.

He lied.

"I'm fine...I'm fine...more theories...let's keep talking, this is good."

"Okay, well, knowing what we know from the past encounters with the military and the fact we know that Tormerdol was researched and engineered there, it's safe to assume that the brothers are heavily involved in all of this. To what degree, I don't know at this point. I do know this: I like Phillip, Jr. as the prime suspect considering we just found his brother dead at home," said Dobson.

"I agree. Everything points to Phillip, Jr. turning on his brother, probably over a dispute concerning their involvement with the military," Martin said, adding credence to the theory posed by Sheriff Dobson.

".....This is pathetic!! You clearly need my help!"

The voice roared out from the dark void, agitated and impatient. The shock wave quaked the inside of Whittaker's mind. He grasped both sides of his head with his hands, squeezing tightly in a vain attempt to push back the pain. The mental tremors were still echoing in a traumatic ripple like a large rock dropped violently into a small pond. The pain was intense and out of pure defense, Whittaker yelled back, "NO!", causing everyone on the block to turn his way.

The sound in his head went deathly quiet and his pain dissipated. Sheriff Dobson motioned for Deputy Martin to go around and assure everyone that the FBI agent was fine and not to be worried.

Dobson knelt to face Whittaker, who was currently doubled over.

As Martin returned to the group, Whittaker looked back up and was eye to eye with Sheriff Dobson.

"Son, this day has been nothing but hell, and I know we haven't known each other long, but it doesn't take a stellar career at the FBI to see that you are holding onto something that is tearing you apart. We see it. Let us help you if we can," the sheriff said, showing a side of real concern for the young agent.

Whittaker rubbed his eyes while finally getting back to his feet. He paused, looking at the other three men in succession, before nodding in agreement to talk.

"Did any of you happen to hear anything about me or my time at the bureau these past few years before my arrival here in Henderson?" he asked.

Martin and Harkins shrugged, not knowing anything

relevant.

Dobson quietly spoke. "I made a call to an old friend who has worked adjacent to the bureau for several years. He told me everyone in your department calls you "The Philosopher," because you can seemingly *think* people into making confessions about themselves without evidence."

Martin and Harkins snickered at the nickname.

Whittaker laughed too.

"Yeah, I think that nickname is ridiculous, too. It started two years ago. I was an office guy working cases via the files, only. I hadn't been in the field yet. I had done some time in the BAU and I would start analyzing case files. You know, breaking down forensics, recognizing patterns that were missed, I was fascinated with the detailed work that went into being an actual FBI investigator. I had given some unique insight into the details of a couple of cases that garnered some positive results, so they decided to take the training wheels off and let me go into the field. I'll never forget that first case till the day I die. We were sent to look into this manufacturer in upstate New York that had been seemingly running an insurance scam where he reported multiple instances of stolen, heavy equipment from his property. He would file a claim and get the insurance money, sell the "*stolen*" equipment out-of-state at a discounted price, then turn around and buy brand new equipment and repeat the process in three months, like clockwork! We couldn't connect the sale of the fraudulent equipment to out-of-state vendors back to the owner, so our only option was to catch him in the act of stealing his own equipment, which meant finding his stash location. My bosses interrogated this guy for hours, trying to get him to give up something...anything...but he wouldn't crack. I was kind of overzealous when they came out of the interrogation room because I asked if I could take a stab at questioning him. Obviously, they laughed at me, the rookie, but said, 'Sure, go for it, kid!' Once in the room, I was completely nervous, and the suspect knew it."

Dobson smiled as he remembered his first interrogation and how similar it was.

Whittaker continued.

"I was flustered, I was asking the wrong questions, I didn't have my notes lined out, I could just feel my superiors' laughing behind the glass as I crashed and burned right there in the room by myself. Then something happened that I still can't coherently explain. From the back of my mind, the words *Tally's Farm* softly echoed to the front of my brain and then escaped from my mouth. The suspect, who had been mocking me and acting like he was checking his watch out of boredom, was now suddenly as white as a sheet. I repeated the words to him, and he wasted no time going on the defensive. He started giving me exposition that was completely unprompted and excuses for why his equipment would be found at that farm, and I just sat there and let him talk. I didn't say a word. Turns out, Tally Farm was an abandoned farm co-op on the New Hampshire side of the state line between Vermont and New Hampshire, which oddly is where I'm from. He would take his equipment there and store it in an old pole barn till he sold it. No one knew because the land is condemned and sits back behind a much larger farm where no one ever goes. He finished talking, and we both sat there in silence, him staring at me, freaked out, and me pretending to be staring off without a care, much like a philosopher pondering the meaning of life. The reality was I was pondering where the voice came from! When, again, out from the back of my mind, the voice said, "*Shipping Container WA65.*" I tell you, gentlemen when I said those words, the man's face went beet red, and he passed out. As it would come to pass when investigators went to the property, they found an old pole barn with brand new locks, and inside was his next run of 'stolen' equipment. He had confessed everything before we even made it out to the property."

SA Whittaker seemingly ended his story prematurely, letting the conversation go awkwardly silent.

The other officers were stunned, curious, and impressed. However, Sheriff Dobson seemed slightly confused.

"What was in 'Shipping Container WA65'?" he asked.

Whittaker was visibly emotional and holding back the pain. He took a few extra seconds before responding.

"The container was butted up against the backside of the pole barn with a couple of large sheets of used plywood leaned up against the doors. A shiny new padlock had to be cut away, and when we opened the container, we discovered his real money-making business. Children. He had been kidnapping children and selling them to black-market purchasers over the Canadian border. We recovered six children that day, ranging in age from seven years old to fifteen years old. Malnourished... cold... scared. It was easily the most devastating thing I have ever witnessed in my life."

The other three men collectively gasped.

"My god, Whittaker," Harkins responded.

Dobson and Martin stoically shook their heads at the story, completely taken aback and not knowing how to react as both men were fathers, themselves, with kids at home.

They all took a moment to let the conversation breathe after such heaviness was relayed, and then the more pressing questions came.

"So, is it safe to say that you've been getting help from a mysterious voice on all of your cases?" asked Dobson. "Even during your time here, you've been hearing it, haven't you?"

Whittaker didn't try and play dumb.

"Every single case I've ever solved, every single suspect I have broken in the interrogation room, the voice has been there guiding me the whole way. And yes...here as well. The only way I can best describe the voice is like this. You walk into a room completely devoid of light... you walk around bumping into things left and right...you can feel the objects, and you have a general idea of what they are, but without light to show you the way, all you are is a fool who thinks he can navigate the dark without bumping into something. The voice has always been my flashlight in the dark. I don't have any explanation as to how or why it happens to me...it just happens."

After all the events of the day that had transpired, as far-fetched as this story was to hear, somehow, the men trusted Special Agent Whittaker and wanted to be there for him to solve this case.

"Do you recognize the voice? I'm just wondering if maybe it's just your intuition or something talking to you, and not like a real person's voice. Does that make sense?" Deputy Martin asked.

"Makes perfect sense, but no, I don't recognize the voice. I don't know whose it is, if it's mine or someone else, or if I'm just losing my ever-loving mind, but, after what I saw in that shipping container and how the voice led me to those kids, I have never once doubted the voice when it speaks. It's just... being here, in this case... the voice has gotten louder, and now I feel it. I don't just hear it. I can feel it. Like it's close. God, I must sound crazy to you fellas," Whittaker said to Deputy Martin, who felt bad for how Whittaker was feeling and having to hold onto this secret for so long.

He empathized with that, carrying around the burden of that fateful night back in 1975. The military had put him into a secretive position, just like Sheriff Dobson in 1963, and now being able to talk about it felt freeing and amazing.

As the three men continued to talk, at the bottom of the hill, a beat-up service van pulled onto the street, circling around and facing back out from the end of the street where it came. It came to a stop and the back doors opened from the inside. There was no light from within, and the back of the truck looked like a mobile, dark void. It caught the attention of Deputy Harkins who instantly recognized the truck from earlier.

"Uhhh, guys, speaking of crazy...that's the truck I saw at Tranquil Meadows!"

All four men came out from the backside of the patrol car where they had been huddled the past couple of hours. They fanned out, walking slowly in the direction of the service truck that was waiting at the bottom of the hill with its back panel doors open, not knowing what the next few moments would hold.

From the darkened void of the truck, a small figure emerged, stepping out of the back of the truck onto the street, eerily sauntering toward the men. As she got closer, the officers could see her thin frame and disheveled hair. She was wearing a patient's gown that was dingy in appearance, just like the other two "patients" from earlier.

She walked with no shoes on and appeared to be carrying something in her outstretched hands. At the sight of her holding something, all the officers in front of her drew their firearms and began yelling for her to drop what was in her hands and get on the ground. She did not comply and kept coming toward the men in her slow approach.

"Does "The Philosopher" still want my help?"

The voice wasn't as forceful this time, and the realization finally hit Special Agent Whittaker that the voice was definitely real and not coming from his own psyche. The question now became, 'Who is the voice?'

Whittaker started making his way toward the girl, calling for everyone to lower their weapons. Sheriff Dobson and his deputies were on his heels, echoing his requests for the weapons to be lowered and to back away from the girl. Whittaker walked down the middle of the street, passing all the officers who had ducked behind their cars for cover and stepping under the police line stretched from one light pole to another across the street.

In the distance, the beat-up service vehicle had closed its doors and taken off around the corner of the next street and out of sight.

As the girl in the patient's gown got closer, Whittaker could see that was she had in her hands appeared to be a folder of some kind with a big red bow tied around the edges. The girl had a crooked smile plastered on her face, and she said nothing as she handed the folder to SA Whittaker.

"a gift..."

The smile faded from the girl's face, and she continued walking at the same pace past Whittaker, who motioned for someone to take her into custody. Deputy Martin stepped forward, taking the girl by her arm, and leading her toward a patrol vehicle, remembering back to that horrible night when a girl similar to this one had killed Ronnie McElroy in such an unspeakable fashion.

Sheriff Dobson and Deputy Harkins stood next to Whittaker as he removed the red bow from the outside. Stamped on the outside was the logo for "Tranquil Meadows

Health." He opened the file folder.

Inside, was a patient's file form filled out for a very familiar name...

Dr. Phillip Killiecrankie, Jr.

Deputy Martin had returned to the other three and was looking at the same thing they were looking at but in confused disbelief. "What could possibly be the point of bringing us this file right now of all times?"

"Because of this right here..." Whittaker turned the folder so the others could see. Under the patient's name, in the box marked "Type of Treatment," scrawled in blood were the words,

"Final Treatment."

"Look at the time that's written down," Whittaker pointed out. The deputies looked at the time on the file and then at their watches.

"10 P.M.? THAT'S FORTY MINUTES FROM NOW!"

Chapter Ten
"Reckoning"

Tranquil Meadows Health
July 21, 1986 | 9:31 P.M.

On the south end of Henderson, down a typically quiet side street off the main road through town, the patrol car of Sheriff Dobson raced at breakneck speed, lights bouncing their colorful beams off the overhead tree branches and nearby homes. The wail of the police siren pierced the night like a specter from the bowels of hell.

Sheriff Dobson and Special Agent Whittaker drove in his vehicle while Deputies Martin and Harkins followed close behind with an abundant force of other police personnel. The row of houses on the south side of the road gave way to a dense tree line, and just on the other side of it sat the property of Tranquil Meadows Health. Dobson and Whittaker squealed into the parking lot, never hitting the brakes. They immediately took note of something very peculiar; the parking lot was empty except for one vehicle.

The mysterious service truck.

The beat-up service truck with the faded Tranquil Meadows Health logo on the side was pulled up directly onto the sidewalk that led up to the main entrance, parked maybe six feet away from the doors. The engine was still running, and the headlights were beaming directly into the front lobby.

Dobson pulled up behind the truck, coming to a stop about twenty yards back. Martin and Harkins parked even with their boss, and all four men exited their respective vehicles, weapons drawn, and defensive positions taken behind their open doors. The panel doors on the truck were wide open and the headlights from Dobson's car revealed that there was no threat in the back section.

Someone must be in the front seat.

"DRIVER! TURN OFF YOUR ENGINE AND EXIT THE VEHICLE, NOW!" screamed Dobson, gun drawn and resolute.

There was no answer.

He called for the driver to comply once again, without any answer.

The hum of the truck had a different feel to it due to the events of the entire day, and the officers were not taking any chances.

Whittaker grew impatient. "We don't have time to wait, Sheriff! You saw the file...10 P.M.! We have to move!"

Sheriff Dobson nodded in agreement and all four men began advancing at a cautious but brisk pace. Steadying their weapons at head level toward both the driver and passenger doors, Dobson on the driver's side and Whittaker on the passenger side, the officers quickly circled out, fully anticipating a suspect encounter.

The cab of the truck was empty. Not feeling an imminent

threat at the entrance of the facility, Sheriff Dobson motioned for the other officers to come forward, followed by a barrage of orders given to groups of three to create a perimeter around the building ensuring no one leaves without being apprehended.

Whittaker, having already opened the passenger door, shut the engine off and was performing a rapid search for clues while Martin and Harkins looked over the back of the truck.

"You guys see anything?" yelled Whittaker, still in the thick of his search.

"We've got fresh blood pooled up in the middle of the bed and then streaked out the back like someone was dragged out of here," Deputy Martin relayed.

"There's also a pile of old, beat-up, used patient's gowns back here, as well. Different designs, though. I think someone's been collecting them," Deputy Harkins theorized. He added one more thought, "Also, the plate on this truck is really, really old. I rubbed away the dirt. It's from at least 1974."

Sheriff Dobson was intrigued by this. He decided to peek inside the cab, hoping to find something worthwhile when Whittaker flipped down the sun visor on the driver's side, and when he did, an old, weathered ID badge in a protective cover fell onto the seat.

Dobson picked it up, and his face sunk as he viewed the picture.

"Martin! Come here!" The deputy wasted no time coming from the back of the truck as Dobson held the ID card to his face. "Recognize him?!"

Martin's mouth fell open as Whittaker came around and joined them.

"Who is it?" asked Whittaker as he checked his watch.

9:37 P.M.

Dobson turned to the FBI agent and handed him the card. It was a picture of a man with a very sizable head that had a large visible scar on the top just past his hairline. He looked very gruff and wasn't smiling. His eyes had an empty look that felt like there was soullessness to them.

Under the picture was the man's name printed over the logo of the facility. Augy Killiecrankie

"This is the man that Deputy Martin and I found dead from a horrible assault out on the country lane after the events of that night at the asylum in '75," the sheriff said.

Whittaker was very surprised by this.

Sheriff Dobson continued, "We had no idea who this man was because there was no record of him existing, so he went into the cold case files as a 'John Doe.' This has to be the truck we heard driving away that night, but if he didn't drive away, then who did?"

"So there's a third Killiecrankie brother? Why was he kept a secret?" asked Deputy Harkins.

Whittaker glanced at his watch again.

9:38 P.M.

"We're running out of time," he said impatiently.

Dobson concurred and instructed two other deputies to

stand guard at the front doors while he, Whittaker, Martin, and Harkins made entry into the facility.

Stepping inside, Harkins noticed right away that the lobby of the facility was very different than earlier that afternoon when he came calling for the Killiecrankie brothers. All the lights were out except for a desk lamp on the front counter, turned on, and facing down at the visitor's sign-in sheet.

As Dobson and Martin shined their flashlights around the room, the state of the lobby was in total shambles. All the chairs, tables, and potted plants had been carelessly tossed and piled up in front of the double doors to the right, blocking entry into the hallway on the other side.

Through the small glass window, the lights in the hallway were flickering like a possessed strobe light which backlit a bloody handprint on the opposite side of the window. On the floor, pictures of the staff members had been thrown to the ground and replaced on the wall by older pictures of staff from the asylum that had all the eyes scratched out and covered with blood.

Sheriff Dobson recognized them immediately and mentioned to the others that these were at the original crime scene in 1975. Someone had gone to a lot of effort to acquire these considering they were taken and cataloged by the United States Military. The double doors to the left were still closed like they were earlier, only this time, written in blood on the door it said:

"visiting hours are ending soon!"

The voice from within Whittaker's head mocked him but wasn't overbearing and violently intrusive like times before.

"...I'm so glad you were able to make it...there's so much for you to see!... I'm just afraid you might be a tad bit late for your appointment with the doctor... better hurry...."

The voice truly wanted Whittaker to experience everything he had to show the FBI agent. This was his show, and Whittaker was the audience.

"We have to go this way," he said, pointing to the left set of doors.

As he passed the front desk, he noticed the visitor's sign-in sheet. The ink pen lying next to it was covered with bloody fingerprints, and there were smears of the crimson liquid all over the page. The last line entered on the page read:

Visitor Name: Special Agent Brandon Whittaker
Reason for visit: Self-Discovery
Doctor's Name: TBD

This is all for me... why? he asked himself.

The others glanced at the page, confused by the text, but knew that now wasn't the time for conversation.

They collectively made for the door.

Opening the double doors led to an immediate influx of chaos. The corridor ahead of the men was in total disarray with furniture from patients' rooms tossed out into the hallway in a belligerent mess, medical equipment smashed and discarded, and the walls and ceiling had holes violently bashed in by cut fists that left a bloody residue on the plaster and surfaces.

They carefully made their way down the hall, searching into rooms as they went, often locating people dressed in doctor's garb yelling and screaming at patients while beating them before darting out from their rooms at the group. The deputies defended themselves, using their firearms to put down the incoming attackers, adding to the body count in the hallway. It was absolute pandemonium.

Halfway down, the hallway had two consecutive sets of double doors that had been heavily damaged and blown open revealing a cafeteria with several tables containing a scattered number of patients in dingy gowns dimly lit by multiple arrangements of lit candles. Each patient was chained to their table, leaving one hand free to feed themselves off a tray that sat in front of them.

The officers slowly entered the room, scanning in every direction for threats. Soft sobbing could be heard from some of the patients while others were vomiting onto the floor. They appeared to have been recently abused, showing fresh bruises and cuts. On a table near the swinging door to the kitchen, a large slab-like tray displayed a heavily filleted carcass of some sort with several sections missing, including the limbs and head.

In the darkness of the room, it was hard to make out what

their mysterious host was serving.

"They were told that they couldn't go back to their rooms unless they finished their dinner...just like we were told...."

"The food on their trays... check them!" SA Whittaker frantically implored the others.

As they made a quick check of the trays, they discovered the horror that lay before them. Human remains, freshly removed from a body, were being given to the patients who were then forced to feed themselves or face the consequences.

At that moment, the door to the kitchen swung open wide and a hefty individual wearing a bloody apron came lumbering toward Whittaker with a very large and very sharp-looking butcher cleaver in his outstretched arms, readying the butcher's tool for massive damage to the special agent.

He swung the cleaver straight down from overhead and Whittaker sidestepped the attack, kicking his attacker with a sidekick straight to the outer portion of his knee, collapsing the joint and sending the man down hard to the ground. While the man was down and writhing in pain, he kept pursuing his attack against Whittaker, who then fired a series of shots, center mast, killing the man instantly.

" The Butcher'... he had only one job at the asylum... my demonstration is not an exaggeration... I hope you're

taking notes, Special Agent Whittaker...."

"Oh god... oh my god!" Whittaker yelled as he started taking patients' trays and sliding them off the table away from them, preventing them from having to eat any more of the human flesh and tissue. Many of the patients cried tears of joy, thankful for Whittaker stopping the bad man from harming them anymore.

They went to continue making their way through the maze of predestined tableaus when Deputy Martin made a grim discovery.

"Sheriff Dobson... I know this patient. She's not a patient at all!" he exclaimed. "This is one of our missing persons!"

Dobson stepped toward the woman, shining a light near her face and confirming what Deputy Martin had discovered. They then cascaded their light around the room, realizing the horrible truth that these were *all* of their missing persons. They were all residents of Henderson County who had been chosen by the conductor of this sordid orchestra, all within the last ten years, to be players on his stage.

Deputy Martin was frantic. "We have to free them now! Come on, guys... help me!"

Whittaker looked at his watch again.

9:46 P.M.

"...tick, tock...."

"We can't stay here with them, Martin. We have to keep going... he's calling for us and the time is now," said Whittaker, making his way out of the room back into the hallway.

Sheriff Dobson walked over to Martin, recognizing the need from his deputy to make good on his vow to track down these missing persons. It was personal for Deputy Martin.

"You stay here with them and make sure no one else comes into this room. When we're finished, we'll free all these people and get them to safety," said Dobson to Martin, who thanked his boss for understanding and assured him he would keep them safe.

Dobson and Harkins followed Whittaker, who was already headed off down the hallway by himself.

"Wait for us, Whittaker!" the sheriff yelled ahead to the FBI agent.

"He wants me. For some reason, this is about me, and I have no idea why. I don't even know who he is!" the special agent yelled in frustration.

"... soon... so very soon...."

After reaching a nurse's station down the hall, various paths were blocked by debris except for one hallway. It felt like the path was already predetermined for this sinister show in blood, and the men had no choice but to follow.

Taking a left and following the hallway around, they entered a back corridor with some lights that were working and some that were not, and the functional ones, flickered and buzzed with popping ballasts due to being heavily damaged. A room down on the right had a steady, bright light flowing from beyond its doorway, beckoning the three officers to investigate.

As they inched closer to the doorway, a small child darted from the room, fleeing across the hallway to an open room and slamming the door shut. The light in the room then clicked off, with a grotesquely shaped figure emerging from the doorway. He was very tall and gaunt, wearing a doctor's jacket and a stethoscope around his neck. He was walking unconventionally toward the officers, carrying a very long, leather strap that was dripping with blood.

All three stood there, frozen by the visual of the unnaturally tall person before them, who swayed from side to side, slapping the strap against the wall and ceiling before hunkering down and breaking into a dead sprint toward the men.

They each unloaded their firearms on the incoming attacker who quickly fell to the ground, convulsing and fighting for air as his lungs filled with blood from the wounds he sustained.

Deputy Harkins knelt beside the man, tugging on one of his pant legs that had shuffled up in the death fall.

"Stilts?" he asked, very confused as to why this person was walking on stilts.

"Dr. Morrison Killiecrankie always seemed so tall to me as a child... like a giant spider with an unnatural fondness for his leather strap... because of that strap we

called him 'Spanky'...."

"Morrison was 6"7, Harkins," replied Whittaker pushing past the deputy and making his way into the room the man came from.

Dobson and Harkins followed.

Whittaker flipped the switch, turning on a massive overhead medical lamp that blazed the room in a sterile, hospital-type glow. On the floor lie the bodies of two military personnel members who had been stripped of their coats and whipped to death by the leather strap the man on stilts was carrying. Strips of their skin had been beaten away from their chests and backs, and their military rankings from their coats had been physically embedded into their chests directly over their hearts, leaving a trail of blood from the wound that pooled up on the floor over their shoulder.

"Majors Robinson and Powers..." said Whittaker, instantly recognizing the dead military men.

"Did you know them personally?" asked Sheriff Dobson.

"No, sir. I knew their missing persons' files," Whittaker said, coldly. "They both went missing within two weeks of each other, along with a large collection of redacted, highly classified Pentagon files. We never knew what the motive was... now we know."

"... you're getting closer...."

Special Agent Whittaker felt an aggression form inside, and it propelled him to push forward. The voice that had been in his head all these years as a beacon of light in the dark was now the cause of all the darkness. It was time to come face-to-face with the monster within.

He continued through the brightly lit room, exiting through another door that led him to a short hallway. He followed it down, around the corner to the right, leading him into the blocked-off corridor from the main lobby.

Standing at the end of the hallway, was a woman dressed as a nurse in a classic nurse's outfit. Deputy Harkins, standing behind Whittaker, lightly gasped, then leaned forward and whispered to Whittaker, "That's the girl from the receptionist desk earlier...."

Whittaker looked down at his watch.

9:59 P.M.

One minute to spare for the appointed time.

Without hesitation, he casually approached the woman dressed as a nurse. With Dobson and Harkins following closely behind, Whittaker never took his eyes off the woman, locked in an exchange of direct eye contact with the girl who never once shifted from her position in the hallway and smiled the entire time.

Whittaker was now only two feet in front of the woman as he slowed his steps and finally broke his stare down to observe her features.

Her face was pale and her hair that was tucked under a

nurse's hat was stringy and thin. She appeared very thin and the clothes she wore seemed to have been just draped over her rather than fit her properly as her scrawny legs trailed down from the skirt she was wearing to a pair of nurse shoes that were about a size too big for her. Two deep hand pockets adorned the front of the outfit, and stitched onto the outside of the left pocket was "Nurse Rucker."

Whittaker looked at the name tag, then back to the girl's face, whose smile was cracking, obviously forced, as a single tear she desperately held onto escaped down her right cheek. This woman was being forced to play a role in this dark production.

"I believe I have an appointment," said Whittaker to the young girl, who nodded and led the three men into an open door to her right that looked like a conference or meeting room.

As they followed, Sheriff Dobson leaned in and whispered to Whittaker, "Nurse Abigail Rucker was reported missing by her family in 1962. We never filed an official report because Phillip Killiecrankie, Jr. told authorities she had been temporarily relocated by his father, Phillip, Sr., for medical follow-ups with out-of-town patients and had documentation to back it up."

"... so many lies by the Killiecrankie family... mother deserved better...."

"His mother..." Whittaker softly whispered, now realizing

that everything he had been shown to this point was more than just some tale of reckoning. It had drifted over the lines of revenge and anger into the realm of a personal vendetta where only a dark, insidious restitution would satisfy the burning feeling of agonizing emptiness perpetuated by the Killiecrankie family.

The young girl led the three men into the conference room, through a door that read "Private Testing Area," into another hallway that passed several observation rooms on both sides of the hall with large glass panels. In each room, two, sometimes three people were bound in straight jackets, screaming and pleading to be rescued.

Being the small town that Henderson, Kentucky is, Sheriff Dobson and Deputy Harkins recognized a few of the people in the room and pieced together that this was the real staff of Tranquil Meadows Health, locked away out of sight, out of mind, so that they couldn't interfere with the plan set forth by the mysterious voice in Whittaker's mind.

The special agent was lost in thought as he mindlessly followed the girl down the hallway, his brain racing in the hope of ascertaining the identity of the faceless voice inside his head. For so long now, this helpful voice guided him along the road of success and was now taking him through a much darker detour. Whoever he was, he carried pain and suffering that had been administered a long time ago to him via the Killiecrankie brother's savagery, and the time for retribution was sounding its chimes on the grandfather clock of his life.

This person, the voice in the void, had to have been a

patient at the asylum and had to have been suffering for a long time. Whittaker thought back in his mind over all the files he had read on this case, and that's when the lightning bolt struck his temporal lobe, sending a shock wave through his memory and placing him outside the asylum, holding a patient file and explaining it's meaning to Sheriff Dobson and Deputy Martin.

"...look at the patient name... H7-423... 423 experiments...."

Just as he realized who was behind the entire plot, the young girl, still forcing a smile, stopped and turned to the three men and said, "Patient H7 will see you now."

She motioned toward a separate observation room that had characteristics different from the other rooms.

The window was made of industrial-strength glass and the access door was a steel door with a wheel mechanism in the center used for securing entry, much like attributes found on a submarine. The lights in the room were turned off, creating a sight in the doorway that was reminiscent of the dark void within Whittaker's mind. They started to move toward the door, unsure of what was about to happen, when the young girl softly reached her hand out and placed it on Whittaker's chest just above his heart.

"Only you. Patient H7 will free the others in the locked rooms, but only if you go alone."

Whittaker reached up and placed his hand over the girl's hand, turned to Sheriff Dobson, and said, "Get these people out of here. It's me he wants..."

Sheriff Dobson and Deputy Harkins protested with their

eyes but knew that this was the only way. In the short time they had known the FBI agent, they had developed trust and knew that the special agent had a better understanding and grasp of this unknown chaos than they possibly could.

Dobson took the girl by her hand and led her away down the hallway to the other rooms. The doors were still locked. Whittaker turned toward the dark room in front of him and carefully stepped inside. When he did, all the doors in the hallway unlocked and swung open at the same time. The cries and pleas of the imprisoned staff members echoed off the walls of the hallway, rippling their pain and suffering as Dobson and Harkins led them out of the building.

"... close the door...."

Whittaker complied, pulling the heavy steel door shut, and wrenching the locking wheel mechanism fully until it stopped spinning. The room's silence was deafening, and the immediate loss of sound began to make his ears vibrate as their audio matrixing tried to decipher the nothingness.

After a few seconds of adjusting to the sound loss, the sensation settled and the empty space was filled with the sound of a heart monitor that had a steady beep. Whittaker was now living out his analogy of being in the dark. The voice in the void brought him here without a flashlight, and the special agent would have to navigate it himself.

He carefully, and slowly, made his way around the room

toward the sound, bumping into random objects he could mildly identify through his senses.

After a few moments, he was within inches of the monitor which had its display blacked out. He felt for the cords, which he then followed that led to the rails of a patient's bed. On the bed, the cords were attached to a person that he could feel was in a patient's gown. At that very moment, the lights in the room came on full beam, staggering him backward as he tried blocking the lights with his hand. His eyes felt like they had initially been burned out, but after a few seconds, they adjusted, and he was finally able to see.

The room was a modified testing space with many different medical instruments set up around the perimeter and a chemical worktable equipped with hot plates, boilers, and gas valves amidst the various beakers and flasks filled with unidentifiable liquids. In the corner, below another completely dark observation window, the patient bed was set up with a man lying upon it, arms and legs bound by medical harnesses, with a series of lead wires running from the patient's head and chest to an unusually large ECG machine.

The man appeared to have been suffering some major trauma as of late.

As Whittaker moved closer, he immediately recognized him as the younger man he had seen in older photos.

Dr. Phillip Killiecrankie, Jr., son of the founder of Western Kentucky Rehabilitation and Sanatorium, Dr. Phillip Killiecrankie, Sr., was visibly older, but certain aspects of his face remained youthful.

He was asleep, clearly having been heavily sedated. Whittaker tried to wake up the bounded man with no luck, and as he did, a light turned on from the other side of the observation glass in the room just in front of him.

Standing prominently in the orange glow of the small room was a man in a beat-up service uniform wearing a dark, thick jacket and fingerless leather gloves. His face was covered with a unique metal mask that covered the entirety of his mouth and nose and the majority of his jawline. His head was completely devoid of hair, except his eyes brows, which were faint in color and thin in volume.

Peering out over the mask were two very dark eyes that were locked onto SA Whittaker, who could feel the sting of their gaze upon him. The faceless voice in the void was now given a physical identity.

Whittaker had been waiting for this moment, but not nearly as long as his new acquaintance.

"I've been waiting a long time for this moment, Special Agent Whittaker...."

the man on the other side of the glass said into Whittaker's mind.

Whittaker stepped around the end of the patient's bed, getting closer to the glass.

"Patient H7, I presume? We have a lot to talk about, I suppose."

"Indeed, we do."

"423... the designation on the paperwork from your file. Experiments? Treatments? Torture?"

The man laughed.

"The number of times it took to make me what I am."

"And what are you, exactly?"

The man raised his hand, holding out his thumb and then flicking it upwards. The switch on the ECG machine behind Whittaker flipped up, turning on the machine. Its heavy hum wafted out into the silent space.

"I'm the next step in human evolution."

Whittaker was surprised and impressed by the display of the man.

"You just turned that machine on. How?"

"Pain-Induced DNA Evolution. It's a theory about humans developing special abilities that my father

realized and my half-brothers unwittingly enhanced,"

he said, turning his stare toward the man on the bed.

"Your father? Half-brothers? You mean?"

Whittaker stammered, fully realizing who and what Patient H7 was.

"Yes, all of it. I was conceived to be a lab rat. I was tested and manipulated for personal gain. I was tortured out of spite and perverse pleasure. My life is nothing but misery. My soul is beyond bruised and darkened. I'M NOTHING BUT AN ENDLESS PIT OF PAIN!"

He screamed, raising his hand, manipulating the dial on the ECG machine with his mind, cranking the voltage up sending a flood of electrical current directly into Phillip, Jr. who jerked and contorted in writhing agony on the bed before Patient H7 lowered his hand back, killing the flow of current.

Whittaker had screamed for the man to stop and was now breathing heavily his adrenaline spiking. His skin began to crawl and inside a weird sensation coursed through his veins that he had never felt before.

"Just wait! I can see where your quest for vengeance has come from, I

understand it now. But why go through all this trouble to put it on display? If you're wanting people to know and understand what happened to you, this is not the way!"

"Come on now, Special Agent Whittaker, you disappoint me. I thought you were way smarter than that. I didn't put this all on display for other people to watch. I arranged this for you."

Whittaker didn't respond.

"And I know from your thoughts that you already figured out that little detail."

"Okay, so why me? Why am I here?"

"You're here because I wanted you to see how miserable my life is... how unbearable it was growing up. I wanted you to walk through the horrors I lived through and get a small taste of the agony that is my life. And I want nothing more, right now, than to punish you for the fact that our mother got to see you thrive outside that hell hole with all the luxuries you were handed while I wasted away in a dirty, unsanitary room waiting for the next time our brothers would pull me out to explore their dark, rage-filled desires. I wanted you to feel the betrayal from me as I helped build you to who you are only to

***bring you here and completely wreck your very being.
I WANT YOU TO SUFFER AS I HAVE
SUFFERED!"***

The proclamation rattled the facility causing the foundation to slightly shift and the walls to crack. The industrial-strength glass in the observation window toward the hallway cracked severely. Phillip, Jr. began to stir in his bed, the sedative wearing off. Whittaker was knocked back slightly but remarkably kept his footing in defiance to Patient H7. The words H7 spoke became fixated in Whittaker's mind, and he couldn't fully understand what they meant or possibly didn't want to understand.

"Our mother? Our brothers? What do you mean by that? There's no possible way that we're... it can't be true!"

Patient H7 stood, somewhat dumbfounded, and gave a slight laugh.

"So this is how Phillip, Jr. felt that night when he told me the truth. Wow. I would've sworn that you had figured it all out by now, but I'm guessing your mind is just blinding you to your own truth. I certainly laid it out and made it easy for you. I'm guessing you're not as diligent with your files as you claim to be. None of that matters now. The time for talking is over."

H7 raised both hands slowly in the air. When he did, lights slowly turned on in all four corners of the secured room revealing four individual fans with metal vials attached to the sides. Phillip, Jr. was fully awake now and recognized the vials.

Tormerdol.

He started yanking on the bindings trying to get free. Whittaker helped remove the straps and both men stood staring at the man behind the glass.

"Tormerdol is a nasty-tasting pathogen. I should know, I've experienced it many times. Luckily for me, it no longer affects my system. But for you two, it certainly means death. You know something, Special Agent Whittaker, it makes me a little sad to know that we will never finish this conversation when there's so much more that needs to be talked about. But, life is full of pain and hope, and you have to find your own way through it. I imagine that's what you'll be experiencing real soon when the pathogen is released."

"LET US OUT OF HERE, YOU FREAK!" screamed Phillip, Jr.

H7 didn't' respond to the taunt. He simply stared for a few seconds then spoke.

"A man once told me that the most satisfying way to

watch someone die was by taking away their ability to breathe because it would ultimately take away their ability to think. Panic of death also enhances that inability to think. Let's see how satisfying it is to watch you both die."

He snapped his fingers, and all four fans turned on, with the metal vials of Tormerdol releasing and pushing the pathogen into the airflow. H7, watched on from the observation room, finally realizing his master plan.

The vapor filled the room quickly as the dense pathogen blew out into the space above and then slowly sank to the ground below. Panic set in for Phillip, Jr. as he started banging on the cracked window and trying to force the door open.

Whittaker remained calm. In the front of his mind, all of his training and all of his research began to swirl into a pool of mental resources that he could pull from, and he used that knowledge to formulate a plan to protect himself from the deadly pathogen.

He started thinking about his personal method of investigating, *The Ten Minute Window,* wondering if this was the beginning of his and Phillip Killiecrankie, Jr.'s end and what details would tell of his demise. The information that Patient H7 had revealed before releasing the pathogen was giving Whittaker mixed emotions and confusion. He did not want his final ten-minute window to be the story told of his life and death, so he pushed those thoughts to the back of his mind so that he could focus. He knew he only had a few minutes before the pathogen would devastate his airways and lungs, so he had to think about a way out before his brain function stopped due to lack of oxygen.

More importantly, he remained calm so that Patient H7 couldn't get any satisfaction from watching his hysteria.

My ten minutes start now.

Whittaker quickly searched the room that turned up nothing. As he bent down to check a bin for something to use to break the window, drops of blood began to pour from his nose and mouth. He stood up, lightheaded, and could feel the pathogen start to take effect. Whittaker looked at Phillip, Jr. who was hunkered in the corner, holding his chest and breathing heavily as blood formed in the corners of his mouth. The special agent's vision was starting to fade in and out, and his skin felt like it was on fire. He tore off his jacket and pulled back his sleeves to reveal that his blood vessels were bursting in his arms.

In his weakened state, he started thinking back over all the files he had read on Tormerdol, and nothing he could remember said anything about the pathogen having this particular symptom. He started to stagger, fighting the effects of the pathogen as best as he could when, deep inside his memory, a very important detail about Tormerdol came flooding back. Oxygen. It was enhanced by oxygen and would do its function as long as it was available. Take away oxygen, and the pathogen evaporates.

Whittaker made his way to the workbench in the middle of the room, grabbing the hose for the gas and ripping it away from the valve. The room slowly filled with gas. He reached into the drawer of the bench and found a flint ignitor. Stumbling across the room to the patient's bed, he grabbed the mattress with all of the strength he could muster and lifted it off the bed. He glanced up at the window and Patient H7 stood, briefly watching the special agent using all his intellect and poise in the dire predicament he had placed Whittaker in before slowly exiting the room.

Whittaker dragged the mattress across the room to the corner where Phillip, Jr. was fading fast, sitting down next to him and laying the mattress across the two of them. He stretched his arm out past the mattress with the igniter in his hand and began striking the flint.

Nothing happened right away, and he kept striking the flint over and over until finally, the spark from the flint ignited the gas in the lab, sending a fireball out from the broken valve, that shot out and exploded, blasting debris in all directions, destroying the glass windows on both sides of the room and creating a vacuum that sent fire cascading out onto the walls and the floors.

The building quickly caught fire, and the inferno began monopolizing the oxygen, which in turn eliminated the threat of the Tormerdol. Under the wreckage, SA Whittaker and Phillip, Jr. laid unscathed by the destruction due to the mattress draped across them. Whittaker regained his strength and began pushing the broken debris off of him. Once he cleared the shambles off him, he noticed that the blood vessels on his arm had gone back to normal. He then pulled Phillip, Jr. from the pile. The older doctor was unconscious, and the effects of the Tormerdol trauma caused blood loss.

Whittaker picked him up and lowered him through the broken window onto the hallway floor. He climbed through the open space and then loaded the doctor into a fireman's carry down the hallway. The fire was spreading quickly, and smoke was filtering down the corridor.

At the far end, an emergency fire exit appeared between the flames and the smoke, and Special Agent Whittaker ran toward it, hitting it with all his force, and sending the door flying open. He immediately fell to the ground, knowing the surge of outside oxygen would reignite the fire, which it did, sending a back-draft of fiery energy out the doorway in a spectacular flash of radiance.

Officers who were posted nearby as part of securing the perimeter rushed over to offer assistance, recognizing Whittaker from before. They quickly got both men away from the scene of the inferno, and back to the parking lot where the entire police force of Henderson County had gathered. EMS had already been called due to the nature of the people evacuated who were used by Patient H7 as supporting actors in his malicious retelling of history. Firetrucks blared their alarms in the distance as they made their approach to the burning building.

Sheriff Dobson and Deputies Martin and Harkins spotted Whittaker from across the lot and came running to his side. They helped him over to Dobson's patrol car and set him on the hood as he caught his breath. They watched as EMS workers scrambled to revive Phillip, Jr., who was still unconscious, loading him into the back of the ambulance for immediate transport to the hospital. While police and fire personnel handled the scene, Whittaker recounted the events that happened in the room and the conversation with Patient H7. Each man stood and listened with a surprised expression on their face. When Whittaker was done, Dobson took a breath and then asked him a question.

"Do you trust Patient H7 was telling you the truth and not just playing more mind games with you?

"I told you before that I have never had a reason to go against the things he's said and the things he's revealed to me. I think he is telling the truth," replied Whittaker.

"So then, who does this mean you really are, Special Agent Whittaker?" asked Dobson.

Before he could answer, a patrolman working the scene for the HPD came running up to Sheriff Dobson.

"Sir, you need to come see this! We have two men murdered on the south end of the building outside an emergency exit. It's two of your deputies!"

Apparent victims of the wrath of Patient H7 as he made his escape.

Sheriff Dobson turned back to Special Agent Whittaker who said, "My identity may very well be in question, but there's one thing that certainly isn't. This investigation is far from over."

Sheriff Dobson and his men ran off to investigate the scene on the backside of the burning Tranquil Meadows Health building.

Special Agent Whittaker sat on the hood of the car, watching as the smoke from the building filled the air in the cloudless night sky. The air was starting to cool slightly, and the stars were beaming bright.

As he sat there pondering his very existence and the questions he had about who he was and where he came from, in the pitch-black recesses of his mind, the dark void inched forward and the familiar voice echoed out softly to him once again.

"....maybe we'll finish that conversation after all... see you soon, brother...."

The End

Epilogue

Special Agent Whittaker sat quietly in the chair opposite his boss's desk, waiting for him to return to go over his report from the events that took place in Henderson. The office was big with high ceilings and white walls that were adorned with framed pictures, official citations, and professional achievements spouting a very successful career at the Federal Bureau of Investigation. After a few minutes, Director Aaron Stephens entered the room, closed the door behind him, walked past his large windows that overlooked a courtyard, and took his seat.

He was carrying a rather hefty file that he laid down on the desk as he sat. His demeanor was upbeat which boded well for Whittaker.

"Let me just start by saying that you have done an amazing job on this investigation. Because of your efforts, we not only have our prime suspect in about thirty different cases ranging from kidnapping to murder, but you've also pulled the curtain back on some top-secret government cover-ups that are going to help us tie the thread that connects decades of unsolved crimes. This is outstanding, Whittaker!"

Special Agent Whittaker appreciated the praise but sat in stoic silence before responding, "None of it matters in the long run, Director Stephens. They'll continue to cover it all up like it never happened."

"This is true. Only now, they have to play ball with us. They have to let our division in on some of their dark secrets because of the overlap with our ongoing investigations. Where we had one hand tied behind our back before, we now have the freedom to solve these big cases... in-house of course."

Whittaker rolled his eyes.

Director Stephens came out from behind his desk and sat on the edge directly in front of Whittaker.

"Look, I know it doesn't feel like it now, but this is a huge win for us. Let's try and keep it going in a positive light, okay?"

Whittaker begrudgingly agreed as Director Stephens got up, walked back around to his seat, and said, "Now the real task begins. We need to find Patient H7 and quickly. The military is insistent upon this."

Whittaker leaned forward in his seat. "The military is 'insistent' upon this? What does that mean? We uncover their secret arrangements with the Killiecrankies that created decades of torture and murder, not to mention the multiple efforts to cover up the entire conspiracy, and now *they're* in a position to make demands?"

The blood vessels on his skin began to rupture, and his insides felt like a raging inferno.

"In their eyes, they had a contract that spelled out an assurance of a delivered product, and they want to make good on that contract, regardless of the lines that are blurred from a legality and morality standpoint. We're operating behind the veil of obscured optics, and this is and will always be off the books. That's not my call to make, I just play in this sandbox."

"So, if we track him down, we don't get to put him away; he just gets locked away like some lab rat once again? No, no, he's mine! I'm going after him, I'll get him. HE'S MINE!"

His face was beet red, and the fire inside made blood form in his mouth, and he could taste the copper sensation.

"I know this is very personal due to what you discovered about your past and finding out that he's your brother."

"He's not my brother..."

"...but the way they see it, they paid for a weapon, and they want it back. If we get him, they're coming for him whether we like it or not."

He leaned forward to sign off on Special Agent Whittaker's report. As he held the pen, it quickly ripped from his fingers, flying across his desk and landing in Whittaker's hand who was now sitting back in his seat.

He calmly clicked the ballpoint pen and asked, "Does that mean the military is going to come for me, as well, Director Stephens?"

Author's Note

The inspiration for this story came about in a very unique way. I was initially brought in as a story consultant to a marketing team for a Kentucky-based haunted attraction called Henderson Haunts. When presented with the working concept of Henderson Haunts on a walk-through, the characters and back-story came flooding into my mind. The story demanded to be put into words for the world to read and I was simply the conduit for the lightning strike.

The concept was simple: Patients left behind in an asylum who then begin to run the asylum.

Which led me to a thought: *What happens when the punished become the punishers?*

I wanted to explore what happened in the past to make this dark future and in turn, tell the story of a lifetime of torment.

We can never truly know what, where, and how inspiration will manifest itself, but it is incumbent upon us as creatives to take the opportunity and draw out every ounce of potential we can from the moment. I feel I've been able to do this with this particular story. But who knows... I think Dr. Killiecrankie might have more source material for me in that deep, dark well.

About the Author

One of Brian's strong suits is taking an existing idea or concept and giving it a life that most people would have never envisioned. When presented with the concept of a local haunted house, the characters and back-story came flooding into his mind and demanded to be put into words for the world to read.

From a very early age, his love for writing fiction was molded by the continued presence of wonderful English teachers that showed him the power of literary visions through creative writing with such classics as "The Legend of Sleepy Hollow", "Beowulf", and "The Rhyme of the Ancient Mariner." His love for writing has only grown exponentially throughout the years and has expanded into non-fiction work with his online movie blogs.

When not writing, recording audio content, or playing tabletop games like HeroScape and HeroQuest, Brian Sumner enjoys spending the rest of his time with his beautiful wife, Crystal, and managing the wackiness of their three kids and one crazy grandson.

To stay up to date with Brian and his work, go to:

www.brianjsumner.com